Tails of Gus & Fanny

The Barn

Dedication

This book is dedicated with love to our cats and our families. And I would also like to add a special thank you to my daughter Emily. Her thoughts, pointers, questions, and encouragement were invaluable to me in the writing of this book.

Acknowledgments

Written by Patti Truedson Higgins

Illustrated by Teresa Weismann Knight

Edited by John Knight

dba PahPahTango Productions

PahPahTango@yahoo.com

ISBN-13: 978-1499160246

ISBN-10: 1499160240

Prologue

Patti Truedson Higgins and Teresa Weismann Knight aren't through with the story of Gus and Fanny. Ideas and questions just keep flying back and forth between author and illustrator. Questions like: The cats need a new home, so why not move them into Gus's barn? What will their cats' days and nights be like living in that barn? Who will the cats meet? Will Gus and Fanny become friends or enemies?

Patti asked Gus those questions as he sprawled like a limp dishrag across her lap. Teresa asked Fanny while Fanny ate and purred at the same time. The cats were both of little and immense help. Some of their stories are true; some are fabrications. All are embellished.

Come along with Gus and Fanny as they continue their saga.

The Domain of Gus
Master Guard Cat

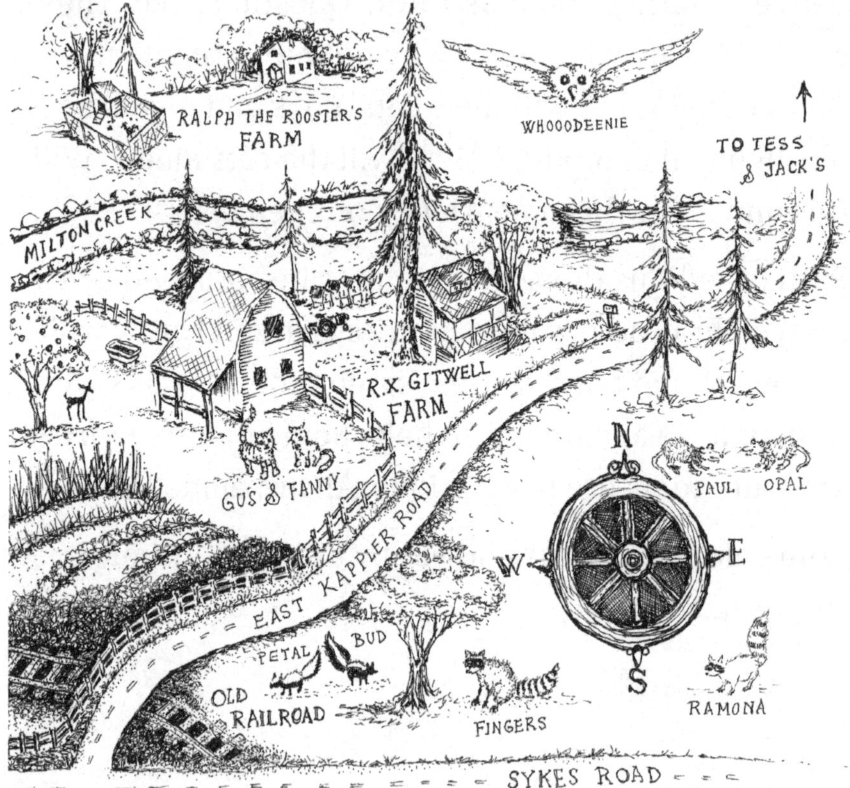
RALPH THE ROOSTER'S
FARM
WHOOODEENIE
TO TESS
& JACK'S
MILTON CREEK
R.X. GITWELL
FARM
GUS & FANNY
PAUL
OPAL
N
W
E
S
EAST KAPPLER ROAD
PETAL
BUD
OLD
RAILROAD
FINGERS
RAMONA
SYKES ROAD

ASBURY ACRES
COYOTES
FAIRGROUNDS
TO PEGGY &
ROB'S

Chapter One

Cock-a-doodle-do!

The muscles in his legs were burning and he was out of breath but he had to keep running. "YOU are The Master Guard Cat of Gitwell Farm!" Gus said to himself over and over. "YOU are a strong tomcat! YOU can do this!" He peeked behind at the coyote hot on his trail but the raindrops splattering his face made it hard for him to see. "I have to keep going! I have to lead this beast away from the little ones! Come on, you mangy coyote, follow me!" Gus sprinted down a steep hill, shot across a busy road, and jetted through the grass of a wide, open meadow. The coyote was gaining on him. "He's going to catch me if I don't make it up that apple tree." But, make it he did. He scrambled up the trunk and into the branches. The coyote came to a screeching halt at the bottom of the tree. He looked up at Gus with his wild, yellow, blazing eyes and threw his snout straight up in the air. He opened his mouth and bellowed:

"COCK-A-DOODLE-DO!"

"What did it say? That's not right! Gus looked down at the snarling, snapping coyote jumping at the bottom of the tree. Coyotes don't crow!"

It threw its head back again and cried:

"COCK-A-DOODLE-DO!"

Gus popped his head up from a bed of soft hay and mumbled, "Coyotes ... don't ... crow." He blinked over and over trying to shake the sleep from his eyes. Something stirred beside him and when he turned he found himself face-to-face with Fanny, the calico cat who called herself Princess Fantas-ti-cat. Fanny, the cat he'd saved and brought to his barn the night before.

"That must have been some dream you were having," Fanny said. She opened her mouth into a wide yawn that showed her sharp white teeth. "Your whiskers were twitching, you were snarling, and your legs were pumping so hard that you stirred up all this dust."

Gus batted at the dust floating in the air. "Well, my dream felt very real."

"Let me to tell you about the dream I just had!" Fanny said. She waved her paw and extended her claws. "Scratch that, mine was a nightmare! First, my mistress Tess brought me to that ancient farmhouse of yours. If that wasn't bad enough, a roaring, rocking, thunderstorm blew through and the old place caught fire." She stood up, arched her back, and shouted, **"Then, I was gnawed on by mice, sprayed by a skunk, chased by giant fire trucks, soaked by pounding rain, and torpedoed with flying tomatoes thrown by a crazy raccoon!"**

Nodding his head up and down in agreement, Gus said, "Well, yeah, it was kind of bad."

"Kind of?" Fanny asked.

"Well, the good news is, we survived and now you're safe in this terrific old barn with me, the Master Guard Cat of Gitwell Farm."

A rooster crowed, "COCK-A-DOODLE-DO!"

Fanny lay back down, rested her head on her paws, and pulled her tail over her face. "A nightmare," she said.

"Okay, yes, a nightmare, but it's all over now," Gus happily purred. "The rooster has crowed. It's time to get up, Princess," he called as he bounded down the bales of hay to the edge of the hayloft. "I'm going out to make my rounds. Peggy relies on me to patrol the place. Why don't you come with me?"

"Who's Peggy?" Fanny mumbled into her tail. "Oh, never mind. I remember Peggy. She's YOUR mistress."

A rooster crowed again, "COCK-A-DOODLE-DO!"

"Sheesh!" Fanny said and got up to look around. *So! This is what the inside of a barn looks like,* she thought. *Gus thinks this one is extra special, a historical monument he told me (whatever that means).* She was standing on a huge stack of hay bales up near the top of the barn. Down below, on the wooden floor, she saw a red tractor, a shelf cluttered with tools, and more tools hanging from pegs on the wall behind it. She glanced up at a hole in the roof. *It doesn't look like anything special to me.* She shook her head. *It's just old.*

"Ralph is a once-in-the-morning crower. Something must be wrong," said Gus.

Fanny watched Gus pacing the floor. The fur on his back was bristled straight up.

"Who's Ralph?" she asked.

"Ralph is my neighbor. He's a New Hampshire Red Rooster."

Fanny growled. "Oh." She settled herself back down on the hay and stretched out. "I know what a rooster is . . . it's a chicken . . . which is a bird." She licked her lips. "I just have never heard of a New Hampshire Red

Rooster."

"Well, Ralph is a good friend and I'm pretty sure something must be wrong so I'm going over to his farm and check on him. Why don't you come with me? Aren't you ready for a little adventure?"

"You go ahead and see about Ralph, your rooster-bird friend. I think I'll just catch a few more winks."

"Suit yourself," said Gus. "But if Fingers or any of the rest of his gang of raccoons come up here, I suggest you hide."

Ralph crowed again, but this time it was more of screech than a crow.

"Is Fingers the smart aleck, tomato-bomber raccoon I met last night?" Fanny yowled.

"That's Fingers, all right."

"And, Fingers belongs to a gang of raccoons?"

"There are at least six of them."

"Wait, WAIT! I'm coming," Fanny yelled. "I think six raccoons are more than I'd like to deal with right now. Not that **this cat** couldn't handle them."

Gus paced the floor. "Well, come on if you're coming!"

Fanny tossed her head, sashayed across the hayloft, slithered down the ladder, and glided across the barn floor to Gus.

I've never met a cat quite like her highness, Princess Fantas-ti-cat, before, Gus thought gawking at her. *Sheesh!* He jumped up on the ledge of an open window and hopped through. “Follow me and oh watch your step, Princess," he called over his shoulder. "There used to be a couple cows living here. Be careful you don’t step in any of the cow-pies they've left behind."

“What is a cow-pie?"

Gus laughed. "Let's just say cows don't use a litter box."

"Oh, eewww!"

Rounding the corner of the barn, the farmhouse came into view. Gus gasped. The back porch and kitchen walls were gone, burned to the ground. The bedroom windows were broken and streaks of black soot spread out over the walls above them. The roof was cradling a huge fir tree that the storm winds had hurled at the house. Gus cringed remembering, how he ran through the yellow flames trying to save Fanny and escape the house.

Fanny nudged him. “Is that a tear in your eye, big fella? Don’t worry. It's not so bad." she said. "Your people will have it fixed up in no time. Trust me. Humans always scurry about after storms blow through and make everything good as new."

Ralph crowed again.

Gus shook his head. "Something is definitely wrong. Come on, Fanny, I'll introduce you to Ralph.” He trotted away.

Good grief, she thought. “Okay, Master Guard Cat, I'm coming. Wait!" Fanny yowled. *I can’t believe I’m going to check on a rooster named Ralph.* “WAIT!”

Chapter Two

Whoooo Whoooo!

The cats ducked under a metal gate and zipped across a mowed hay field to a barb wire fence. Gus hopped between the strands of the thorny wire and waited until Fanny was safely through before continuing down a narrow dirt path. The path took them deeper and deeper into a cool dark forest of towering fir, maple, alder, and dogwood trees. The trees were wrapped in blankets of soft green moss and their tangled branches seemed to be in a battle for the sunlight above.

Fanny stayed close to Gus trying not to lose sight of his tail in the tall weeds that hung over the path. Then, POOF, they broke out into the light of an open meadow.

“COCK-A-DOODLE-DO!” Ralph crowed.

The cats followed the trail across the meadow and down a steep cliff to a creek. Gus hopped from rock to rock to the other side.

"Wait, WAIT!" Fanny called after Gus. "I’m a cat! You don't really expect me to cross this creek!"

Gus hopped the rocks back to Fanny. "I’m a cat, too, and I just did it . . . twice. It's easy."

Fanny whined, "Cats don't cross raging waters! Besides, what if I slip?"

"You won't slip."

Still whining, she said, "What if I fall in? The current will take me to the ocean. I could drown!"

Gus looked at the shallow, slow-moving creek and shook his head. "Trust me, you won't slip." He hopped out on the first rock. "See the tops of the rocks are dry, not slick." And then he hopped on over to the other side of the creek. "See, piece of cake."

Fanny looked at the smooth dry rocks jutting out of the water then up at Gus.

Gus winked and said, "Easy peasy."

"I can't believe I'm about to do this." She started shivering and shaking. *Here goes nothing,* she thought. She hopped to the first rock, then the second, then the third but her hind foot drug in the water as she hopped to the shore. She shook her paw wildly. "I hate being wet! I could have drowned!"

Gus touched Fanny nose to nose then ran on.

Fanny bristled and hissed, "How dare you?" She bolted past him, crested a hill and halted at a white picket fence that wound around a yellow house.

Gus caught up and stopped alongside her and said, “I’m really sorry I touched your nose with my nose.”

“NEVER touch me nose to nose without my permission! For your information only sweethearts do that! And, I’m not your sweetheart!”

“I’m REALLY sorry,” said Gus.

“But, I’m probably the prettiest cat you’ve ever met, so I understand.”

Gus shrugged. “Sorry.”

“Humph!”

“Anyway,” Gus said, pointing. “This is Ralph’s farm! See the little brown building next to the red barn that is Ralph’s chicken coop? The fenced area around it is a chicken yard. And, see the big New Hampshire Red rooster stomping around inside? That’s Ralph.”

Ralph crowed, "COCK-A-DOODLE-DO," three times in a row.

"Sheesh!" they said at the same time and then crossed the lawn to the pen.

"That’s a lot of racket, Ralph! What’s up?” Gus asked.

Ralph stopped mid-stomp and shot straight up off the ground. "Geez! Don't scare me like that!" He strutted to the fence and nodded toward Fanny.

“Who’s this?”

“Ralph, this is Fanny.”

“Is she your sweetie, Gus?”

Fanny hissed. “I’m not his sweetie!”

"Nah, we’re just friends. She’s staying at the farm with me for a little while. So, Ralph, what’s going on? Why all the crowing? You seem pretty stressed."

"Stressed?" Ralph asked. "Yes, I'm pretty stressed!" He pecked the ground with his beak. "The hens are stressed!" He pecked the ground. "The chicks are stressed!" He pecked the ground. "It has been a stressful night and this morning it's not getting any better!"

"I see you're keeping the hens and chicks inside the coop." said Gus.

Ralph nodded, "I told them to stay in there until I give them the all-clear signal." He strutted in circles kicking at the hundreds of fir cones littering the ground. "The wind tore the roof off last night and the hens became hysterical! They kept saying, 'The sky is falling! The sky is falling!’ Now, Whoodeenie is terrorizing us!"

A shadow crossed over the pen. Ralph croaked,

"COCK-A-DOODLE-DO!" They all ducked. Gus looked up in time to see Whoodeenie, a large barn owl, fly past and land in a tree. The bird swiveled its white, heart-shaped face around, stared at him, and blinked. The fur on Gus's back spiked straight up.

"Whoodeenie has us all spooked! He's been doing that all morning!" said Ralph. He pointed a wing at the house. "No one is home to help us. They all left yesterday before the storm. Please help us! I'm worried about the chicks."

"Tell me about this barn owl, Gus," said Fanny. "I get the feeling he's not one of your friends."

"Whoodeenie is a deadly menace!" Ralph yelled.

“Barn owls like Whoodeenie usually hunt at night,” said Gus. “They have excellent eyesight, especially in the dark. They have extraordinary hearing too, I mean they can be flying way up in the sky and hear the slightest rustle or squeak in the plants below and know if it is a mouse or a vole. And, oh man, their massive wings make next to no noise when they fly! If they start hunting you, it’s hard to outsmart them and get away.”

“And, if Whoodeenie reaches down with his sharp clawed talons, grabs you, and flies up into a tree or lands on a rooftop, he’ll try . . . to eat you! A deadly menace!” said Ralph.

Fanny scanned the sky. "Okay!" she said. "So, what you're telling me is barn owls are a lot like hawks and eagles."

Gus and Ralph looked at each other. "Pretty much," said Gus.

“So, why is Whoodeenie flying around hunting during the day?” Fanny asked. “You said he was a night hunter.”

“He didn’t get a chance to hunt last night on account

of the storm," said Ralph. "He's plenty hungry today."

"Oh," Fanny said.

A huge flock of shiny, blue-black crows suddenly filled the sky. The uproar of caw-cawing was as loud as fireworks on the Fourth of July . The crows swooped together and landed in a tree next to the house. The same tree Whoodeenie was in. The tree came alive with the quivering and shaking of flapping wings as the birds hopped from branch to branch. Gus snickered. "You have to watch this, Fanny."

"Why? What's happening?"

"Just watch," said Gus.

Whoodeenie swiveled his big face back and forth watching and warning the crows to stay away. But the crows just kept coming in closer and even pecked at him. Whoodeenie finally had enough. He stretched out his wide wings and flew out of the tree. The crows didn't seem to be satisfied with Whoodeenie simply leaving the tree. They followed after him, taking turns flying right in his face. Whoodeenie let out loud, high screeches. He pecked at them but they were too quick and always veered away. The raucous flock of crows flew higher and higher into the sky then disappeared over the hill, taking Whoodeenie with them. It was suddenly quiet on the farm.

Ralph let out a sigh of relief as he watched the owl fly away.

"Why were the crows being so brave and bothering the owl so much?" Fanny asked.

"The crows don't want Whoodeenie to hunt here where they raise their babies!"

"Oh," said Fanny. "Babies."

Chapter Three

Buck Buck Buc-kawk!

Gus climbed a tree to get a better look at the chicken coop." Geez, Ralph, the storm picked up the roof and flipped it over. There's not much I can do about it."

"Are you sure?" Ralph asked.

"Sorry old pal, I have paws. I need a pair of hands for this job." As luck would have it, just as Gus was saying that he caught sight of two raccoons waddling toward them. "Hey! Fingers!" he yelled.

Ralph and Fanny looked behind them and saw two raccoons. "Oh, good grief!" said Ralph. "It's that gangster raccoon, Fingers and his brother Handzie. Ohhhh."

"Hey, Ralphie boy," said Fingers, He pushed his snout through a hole in the chicken wire fence and said, "Boo!"

"COCK-A-DOODLE-DO!" Ralph crowed then ran in circles inside the chicken yard.

Gus hopped to the ground. "Geez, Fingers! You scared Ralph half out of his wits."

"Ha! He scares easy." Fingers slapped the raccoon standing next to him on the back. "The boss sent me and my brotha Handzie out ta see what was what afta that big ol' storm ripped through. With all the crowin' Ralphie's been doin' I figured I'd find youz here, Gus." He waddled up behind Fanny and whispered in her ear, "No more tomatas." He twirled his gold pinkie ring and held up his empty hands. "Mosta that skunk spray youz was wearin' yesterday's gone." He laughed and sniffed at her fur. "Youz don't stink no more, Princess." Fanny growled. He backed away still holding up his empty paws.

Fingers snickered. "Did it work, or did it work? Youz can thank me later, Princess." He threw his head back and sang, "But just rememba . . . love stinks."

Fanny snarled, "He's NOT my sweetheart!" *Love stinks?* She sniffed her fur.

"FINGERS, we need your help with this coop roof. Would you climb up there and flip the thing over?" Gus asked.

Fingers and Handzie waddled over for a closer inspection. He cracked his knuckles. "This is gonna cost youz guyz!" He looked in at Ralph. "I could eat a couple eggs. Hee hee hee!"

"Ralph stretched tall, bobbed his head toward the raccoons and crowed, "COCK-A-DOODLE-DO!"

"FINGERS, don't be stressing Ralph any more than he already is!" said Gus. "I have plenty of kitty kibble to share!"

"Just soz youz do," said Fingers.

"Fingers, you sound more and more like a gangster all the time. We won't be able to understand a word you're saying if you keep this up," Gus said.

Fingers slapped Gus on the back. "I knowz. Ain't it grand? If I wanna move up in the gang I gotta walk-the-walk and talk-the-talk." He strutted in a circle.

"Fingers is copying Tony's cousin, Knuckles," said Handzie.

"What? Tony has a cousin?" Gus asked.

"Who is Tony? Who is Knuckles?" Fanny asked.

Handzie waddled over next to Fanny. "Tony's the boss. He runs things. He's real smart! Knuckles is Tony's cousin. He hitched a ride in a big truck all the way from New Jersey. He's a real gangster."

Finger's shrugged and climbed to the top of the coop and wrestled with the roof. "This here's a two raccoon job! Handzie! Get up here and give me a hand!"

Fingers and Handzie flipped the roof back into place

and climbed down from the coop. Fingers brushed himself off and then held his right paw up to the light and twirled the gold ring around his pinkie finger. Handzie did the same but twirled an imaginary ring. Fingers shook his head at Handzie and then waddled over to Gus and patted him on the back. Handzie did the same.

"Stop copyin me, Handzie!" said Fingers.

"Stop copyin me, Handzie!" said Handzie.

Fingers pushed Handzie's shoulder. "Knock it off!"

Handzie pushed Fingers' shoulder. "Knock it off!"

"Youz better stop it!" said Fingers

"Youz better stop it!" said Handzie.

Fingers shook his head. "Our work is done here," he said. "Tony says ta get back real quick-like."

"Our work is done here," said Handzie. "Tony says ta get back real quick-like."

Fingers pushed Handzie's shoulder and started waddling away. Handzie hurried to catch up with Fingers and pushed Fingers' shoulder. Fingers pushed Handzie and ran ahead. Handzie ran to keep up.

“Gangster raccoons," Fanny asked? Gus shrugged.

Ralph marched up a wooden plank and disappeared into the chicken coop. Moments later he emerged, followed by four hens and a dozen baby chicks. Rooster, hens, and chicks strutted around the pen on their skinny legs pecking at the ground, making happy clucking sounds. Ralph came to the fence and said, “Thanks for coming. Thanks for being a good friend, Gus.”

“Sure thing,” Gus said. “What are friends for if not to support one another?”

“Yeah!” said Ralph.

Gus looked at Fanny and said, “Race you back to the barn!” Fanny tore out spraying gravel behind her. “Beat you!”

Chapter Four

Growl Growl

“Gus! Gus! Wake up! I hear something!” said Fanny. It had been warm and sunny in the barn when she’d fallen asleep. Now it was dark. She nudged him. "Guuusssss!"

Gus's head skyrocketed up like a submarine’s periscope from deep beneath the sea. A piece of straw hung from his chin. "What is it, Fanny?"

Growls, hisses, grunts, and thumping sounds were coming from the floor of the barn. Gus crept to the edge of the hayloft and looked over. There stood Fingers shoulder to shoulder with a ‘possum, both of them glaring at Bud, the skunk. Gus tilted his head and tried to make sense of what was happening between his three friends.

Fanny padded silently up beside Gus and whispered, “Is that Fingers?”

“Yes.”

“What about the other two? Who are they?”

“Well, the skunk, that’s Monsieur Bouquet, but we just call him Bud. He used to live in the basement of the old farmhouse.”

“Is he the skunk that sprayed me last night during the storm?”

“Yes, that was Bud, but he felt terrible about it. He said he didn’t mean to puff. He said it was an accident.”

“Humph!” Fanny said.

“The other one with the rat-like tail, the one swaying side-to-side with his lips snarled back and growling, that’s Paul, he’s a ‘possum. He’s usually a pretty quiet fellow. Actually, I hardly ever see him,” Gus said.

“Well, he’s certainly here tonight and he’s not being quiet either,” said Fanny.

Bud was cowering before the raccoon and opossum. "Don't make me puff. I don't want to puff," he said. He nervously gritted his teeth. His little legs shook as he stomped his feet and his black and white skunk tail rose higher and higher.

The pitch of Paul’s ‘possum growl was also rising higher and higher until . . . he keeled over.

Fingers poked Paul and then twisted his gold ring. "Buddly! Ya stink bomber!" he snarled. "Youz killed him."

Now Bud's tail stood straight up. He shook his head

side to side. "I, I, I," he stammered. "I didn't mean to kill him."

Fingers picked up the opossum's rigid arm and let go. It dropped back to the floor with a thud. "Yup, Buddly, Pauly's a goner."

Bud reached out and touched the 'possum with his paw. "Oh, my," he murmured.

Gus jumped from the hayloft. "Bud, Bud calm down." He glared at Fingers. "What is going on here?"

"Geez!" said Fingers. He poked the 'possum with his foot. "Pauly here and me, well, we was havin' a disagreement with the stink-maker."

Gus put his face up to the 'possum's. "Bud, Paul is still breathing. You didn't kill him. 'Possums play dead when they are upset. They even call it playing 'possum. Didn't you know that?" Gus nudged Paul with his hind foot and sat down. "What's this all about?"

"We was tellin' Buddly he ain't welcome ta stay in the barn with us this winter," said Fingers.

Bud dropped his head and looked at the barn floor. "I won't take up much room. I'll be very quiet and I won't bother anybody." He peeped up at Gus. "You'll hardly know I'm here." He shifted his weight from

foot to foot. "I'd like to spend the coming winter in that corner." He pointed, "under the barn."

Fingers shook his head, “Youz a skunk and skunks stink.”

"I don't stink." Bud sniffed his tail. "Do I, Gus?"

"Well," said Gus. "You do usually have a bit of an odor."

"I won't be puffing. I'll be sleeping all winter," said Bud.

"Skunks don't hibernate," said Fingers.

"Mostly we do," said Bud. He hung his head even lower and drew circles in the dust on the barn floor with his paw. “Besides, you’ll be hibernating, too.”

Fingers shook his head. "NEITHER ONE OF US HIBERNATE! And besides, even if youz did, youz might have a bad dream and puff and that would totally stink up the joint.”

Clouds parted in the night sky and suddenly, the light of a full moon came through a hole in the barn’s roof and landed on Paul like a stage spotlight. Everyone turned and gazed at him. It was spooky. First, Paul’s ear twitched, then the other ear twitched, and then he opened his eyes and lifted his head. Fanny gasped.

Bud jumped up and covered the ‘possum's face with kisses.

“Where am I?” Paul asked. He got back on his feet and brushed the skunk away. "Knock it off!"

"Pauly, before youz so rudely fainted, we was tellin' Buddly here, no way's we’re lettin’ a skunk spend the winter in the barn with us," said Fingers.

Paul opened his mouth to say something but snapped it shut because a booming high pitched screech filled the night air. They all looked up at the hole in the roof and whispered, “Whoodeenie!” Then, more frightening than the screeching, there was a dreadful silence. Everyone inside the barn panicked at the sound the owl made as it landed beside the hole in the barn’s roof.

Fanny yowled. She dove off the side of the hayloft and dropped with a perfect cat-on-all-four-feet landing next to Gus.

Gus yowled and arched his back.

Paul froze in place.

Fingers and Bud scurried under the tractor. Fingers grabbed Bud’s skunk tail, held it firmly down, and whispered, “Don’t youz be puffin’ that stinkin’ spray on me.”

Whooodeenie screeched, swooped inside the barn, and back out again in a flash. He perched on the roof and stared at them blinking his big eyes.

Paul fell to the floor with a thud. He rolled over on his back, his feet up, his tongue out, and his eyes closed. He'd fainted again.

In a shaky voice, Bud whispered to Fingers, "Are you sure that's Whoodeenie, the barn owl? If it's Whoodeenie, I could give him a little puff and he'll fly off. But if that's a great horned owl, like Spike . . . well, they aren't scared away by a little skunk puff. "

"It's Whoodeenie, all right. Can't youz tell by the screech? Spike don' sound like that," said Fingers. "Besides, rememba I said no puffin' you smelly stink bomb!"

Bud pulled at the fur on Finger's arm. "Fingers, look! Whoodeenie's got something ... or someone in his talons."

Fingers climbed out from beneath the tractor to join Gus and Fanny. In his deepest, meanest raccoon voice he growled, "We ain't afraid of youz, Whooodeenie!"

Bud climbed out too clicking his teeth and stomping his feet. In his deepest, meanest skunk voice he growled, "I'm not afraid of you either!"

Paul's ear twitched. He raised his head but lowered it back down. He opened his eyes just a teeny-tiny bit and watched the others.

Gus jumped from the floor of the barn to a barrel sitting next to the wall. From there he leaped to the hayloft, then to a beam, high in the rafters of the barn. Fanny followed him. Together they crouched and growled. Whooodeenie swiveled his head to look at them. Gus sprang like an arrow from a bow straight toward the owl leaving Fanny teetering on the beam. Whooodeenie screeched and flew away. Gus climbed out on the roof and yowled, "AND DON'T COME BACK!"

"YAY!" Bud yelled.

"Nice!" said Fingers.

Paul rolled over and stood up. "Phew!"

Fanny watched Gus marching back and forth on the roof. *Show off,* she thought, *handsome though* . . . . She climbed back to the barn floor. Gus followed.

"See everybody," said Bud, "I was scared, but I didn't puff! I'm a brave boy. Paul fainted; he's not a brave boy." He turned to Paul. "No offense, Paul." He turned back to Gus. "Won't you let me spend the winter here with you?"

Fingers mumbled as he waddled to the window. "We ain't done talkin' 'bout this, Bud, oh boy. You might be brave, but I'm not too sure I wanna skunk livin' here with us." He climbed out the window and hollered, "I got places ta go, folks ta see, and things ta do."

Paul nodded to Gus, Fanny, and Bud. "I'm brave when I need to be. It takes a lot of bravery to play dead around a big owl. Anyway, I knew Gus had my back." He bowed. "Now, if you'll excuse me, I too have places to go, folks to see, and things to do." He followed Fingers out of the barn singing, "I've been with cats, raccoons and some mink, but one thing's for sure . . . skunks stink!"

Bud cleared his throat. "Uhm, Gus?"

“Yes.”

“Gus? I really really want to stay here with you. Please, I’ll be so so good,” said Bud.

"We'll figure something out, Bud."

"My stomach is rumbling something awful. I'll be going too," said Bud.

"Well, Master Guard Cat!" said Fanny.

"Well, Princess Fantas-ti-cat, shall we?" said Gus.

The cats leaped through the barn’s open window. "Gus, I understand why Ralph and his brood of chickens and chicks are afraid of Whooodeenie, but why are Bud, a skunk, Paul, a ‘possum, and even Fingers, a big tough raccoon, afraid of him?" Fanny asked. "Surely, they can take care of themselves."

"Don't underestimate Whooodeenie. But, you're right. Those boys can take care of themselves. They don't want Whooodeenie getting comfortable and making his home here because he could hurt their babies just like Ralph's chicks."

"Oh my!" said Fanny.

Gus started across the grass field.

"Wait, WAIT," Fanny yowled. "What babies?"

Chapter Five

Rumble Rumble

Fanny caught up to Gus. She trotted alongside him for a few steps and then stopped and sat down. She watched him cautiously scout the area, his head held high, his ears darting this way and that, listening for danger. "I don't want another adventure," she whined. "I'm tired and I'm hungry and I want to go home." She laid down and put her head on her paws. "I just want to go home. How long have I been here, Gus?"

Gus sat down and scratched at a flea. "You stayed with me in the farmhouse a couple days. Last night the storm blew through, so this will be our second night in the barn."

Fanny didn't respond, so Gus finally said, "I'm hungry, too. Would you like me to go hunt something up and bring it to you? You can wait for me back in the barn?"

Fanny raised her head. "The barn? I don't want to run into Bud, Paul, or Fingers in your barn. What are you going to do about them? Are you going to let them stay in there with you this winter?"

Gus paced in a circle around and around her. "I don't

want to if they are going to be bickering and fighting all the time."

"If I lived there, and it was MY barn, I would chase them all off, especially that raccoon!"

"Fingers? Oh, he's the one I would say yes to above the others. They are all my good friends but Fingers is my oldest, dearest friend."

"Humph!" said Fanny.

"I know Fingers is a gangster raccoon and his gang waddles around bullying their way into nests, houses, barns, sheds, and garages tearing stuff up. They eat pet food and garden crops. They dump over garbage cans and make messes. But Fingers isn't like the rest of them."

"What makes him different?" Fanny asked.

"He only eats other's food if he earns it. He only tears things up if there's a good reason."

"Whatever you say, Gus."

Fanny bobbed her head watching weird birds dart about in the moonlight. "What are those?"

"It's just bats," Gus said. "They're chasing bugs."

"Bats?"

"They're furry little critters. They look kind of like a flying rat. I've tried to catch them. Don't bother. They're way too quick. And, anyway, they won't hurt you."

Fanny settled back down. "Oh, bats, hmmm. So, Gus, how did you meet Fingers?"

"Oh geez, Fingers and I met when I was a kitten and he was a kit. Are you sure you want to hear this story?"

"Yes," said Fanny.

"Well, it was my first night alone in the farmhouse. I found a soft place to sleep upstairs right under a window so I could look out for any danger. I was kind of scared since I was all alone and everything. So anyway, I had no more than closed my eyes when the attic door up in the ceiling burst open, Fingers fell through and landed with a thunderous thud on the floor. It scared the tar out of me! But he didn't know I was there. When I growled it startled him and he tripped and fell down the stairs. He rolled like a ball all the way to the bottom and crashed into the wall. At first he was screaming. Then the crying started. Finally he just moaned. I waited to see if he was going to come back upstairs but he didn't, so I tiptoed down a few steps and asked him if he was okay."

"What did he do?" Fanny asked.

"He sniffled . . . a lot. He rubbed his tail and said it hurt really bad. 'I think I broke it,' he moaned then started howling. I wasn't sure what to do for him but one thing was for sure, I wanted him to stop that howling. So, I ran back upstairs and searched around trying to find something I could use to mend his tail. That's when I found a gold ring sitting on a dresser. I rolled it down to him and told him to put it on his hurt tail."

"Why would he want to put a ring on his tail?" Fanny asked.

"I thought it might make it feel better. He tried to slid it on his tail but it was too small. I was getting ready to cover my ears because I was sure he would start

wailing again, but he didn't. He wiped the tears from his eyes with one hand and held the ring up to the light with the other. He turned it over and over examining it from all sides and then he slid it on his finger."

"Is that the ring he is constantly admiring?"

"Yup! And he's worn it ever since. When he blows on it, rubs it against his fur, and holds it up to the light, and winks, it's our secret signal. He's saying no matter what, we'll always be friends."

Oh brother, Fanny thought. *If I hadn't seen Fingers*

wearing that ring I'd never believe that story! "That's quite a tale, Gus. So, tell me about the 'possum."

"Paul? Geez, I met Paul one night near the garden. I saw the poor 'possum get clipped by a passing car. It sent him flying and then he just laid there, not moving a muscle, sprawled out flat on the road. I felt sorry for him because I was pretty sure he was dead. But then, miraculously, he lifted his head."

"Like he did tonight in the barn?"

"Yes, just like he did in the barn. So, there he was, lying on the road, making no attempt to get up when a pickup truck came barreling up the road in a collision course with the stone still 'possum. He was going to be flattened! I jumped into action. Being the brave Master Guard Cat that I am, I ran to him, grabbed him by the neck with my teeth and tried to drag him off the road. Thankfully, Paul woke up twitching, stammering and stuttering. I still had to prod, paw, and finally claw him to make him move. We both managed to stumble out of the way of the tires as they rolled past."

"Did that really happen?" Fanny asked.

"Yes it did! I checked him over once we were safely off the road a ways. He was winded and probably

bruised, but otherwise okay, that's when he told me his name was Paul.

"So, you saved Paul's life." Fanny said.

"I think if you save someone's life you are responsible for them from then on. And truly, Paul takes a lot of looking after!"

Fanny's stomach rumbled loud enough for Gus to hear. "You know, I wouldn't mind hunting something up for us to eat and bringing it back to you. You must be tired," said Gus.

"No, I'll go with you. I'm probably a better hunter

than you, anyway," Fanny said.

Gus shrugged and walked to an old bathtub full of water. He jumped up on the rim of the tub and lapped up some water. "Do you want a drink? There's fish in the water - it makes it taste really good."

Fanny hopped on the side of the tub and walked all the way around it staring into the water before taking a drink. "And Bud," she asked, "the little stinker, how did you end up with a skunk for a friend?"

Gus hopped down and cleaned his face with his paw. "I found Bud sleeping under the farmhouse one night during one of my routine patrol missions. I was just about to go over and poke him when I recognized his black and white skunk stripes and stopped. He was just a kit, but hey, even baby skunks spray that horrible smelling stuff, so I inched my way back out as quietly as I could. My plan was to let him stay that night and figure out a way to keep him from coming back after he left in the morning, but then I tripped over a pipe and woke him up."

Fanny hopped down. "Bud is your friend even though the first night you met him he sprayed you?"

"That's the thing, Fanny, he didn't spray me. He raised his little head and said, 'I won't puff you.' Bud never

says he sprays, he says he puffs."

"Humph, his puffs are no fun! He puffed me!"

"Accidentally puffed you. He said it was not on purpose."

"Humph!"

"Anyway, that night Bud said to me, 'I puffed at Spike already tonight. I have to make more puff juice before I can puff again.' You should have seen him. He was adorable."

"And who is Spike?"

"Spike is a great horned owl. I'm sure we'll see him one of these nights. Most owls leave skunks alone, but not the great horned. They prey on skunks along with everything else. I climbed a tree one time and found one of their nests. It smelled like skunk."

"So, Bud didn't puff you that night?"

"No, he said I was THE Master Guard Cat who lived upstairs and he would never puff at me. He asked if we could be friends. How could I say no?"

"I'm pretty sure I could say no," said Fanny.

"I don't think it's a bad idea to have a skunk as a friend. It is much better than having a skunk as an enemy!"

"I suppose," said Fanny.

"Well, I let Bud stay in the basement of the farmhouse as long as he followed the absolute rule."

"And the absolute rule is?" Fanny asked.

"Absolutely no puffing under the house, of course."

"But Bud always stinks."

"I know, but I like him."

Fanny sighed and her stomach rumbled again. "Gus, I'm hungry."

Gus's stomach rumbled. "I'm hungry, too. Come on, let's find something to eat!"

Chapter Six

Crunch Crunch

Fanny half-heartedly inched her way across the hayfield hunting for something to eat. She stopped, sprawled on her side, licked her right front paw and sighed. "I wish I was home right now! I wish I was standing in front of my food bowl and that it was filled to the top with crunchy, delicious brown, red, and yellow kibble!" Then she added dreamily, "I would eat and eat until my stomach was so round that I would have to stretch out on the ground and wait for it to digest." She stretched and dropped her head to the ground.

Gus paced around her. "Yeah, what I wouldn't give for a nice bowl of kibble right about now, too."

"Actually, you know what would be even better is if I was eating the tuna fish Tess TRICKED me into stepping into that dreadful pet taxi with."

Gus laughed.

"It's not funny! I just hate when I've been tricked!"

Gus batted her shoulder with his paw. "Peggy can trick me any day of the week if she gives me tuna fish to eat."

Fanny jumped up and batted Gus back. "The problem is I fall for her trick every time. I just can't resist the mouth wateringly good flavor of tuna fish. The temptation is so strong that I forget it's a trick and I crawl inside that horrible cage and, WHAM, she closes the door and I'm stuck. Humph. It's so upsetting! You know?"

"Ah, yes, I understand. Getting into a pet taxi usually means going to that horrible place where you get man-handled and poked with sharp needles." Gus batted Fanny.

"Yes, that place! That horrible place with all the strange smells! My nose goes crazy." said Fanny. "And stop batting me!"

Gus batted Fanny again and laughed.

"I'm warning you, cut it out, Gus!"

Gus pounced at her. She sprung away. He pounced again. She pounced back. There was a blur of paws, claws, and tails but the cats stopped tussling in midair when lights shown moving up the driveway. In a blink, Gus ran toward it.

Fanny was not so eager to investigate. She stood still, watching and listening. When she heard someone calling, Gus-Gus over and over, she relaxed a little. Then she saw a little girl, a tall man, and a black and white dog. *Yikes, a dog!* She thought and then ducked into some tall grass to hide.

When the little girl reached Gus she picked him up and nuzzled his head with her face. "Oh, Gus-Gus, I'm so glad you're all right," she said.

The man reached over and petted Gus and said, "Hey Gus-Gus, ole buddy, you must be starving."

Fanny recognized the smell of the big bag the man had slung over his shoulder. *Kibble!*

The little girl had Gus wrapped in a tight hug and the dog trotting alongside was sniffing and poking at him with its nose.

Once they went inside the barn, Fanny crept close enough to see what they were doing. The dog sniffed everything in the barn, the stub of its tail wagging so fast it made its whole body shimmy. Fanny crept even closer when the man lifted the lid of a big, wooden box and drop the kibble bag inside. She inhaled the sweet scent of kitty kibble and sighed after he ripped off the top of the bag, scooped some into a bowl, and put it on the floor.

"Jessie, let Gus eat his food. The poor cat is hungry."

Gus was struggling to get down. Jessie gave him one last squeeze and kissed his head before dropping him to the floor.

Fanny sneaked into the barn and hid under the tractor.

"Dad, where do you think Fanny is?"

Gus lifted his head from the bowl of kibble. His mouth was full, his jaws crunching. "Fanny," he mumbled, sending crumbs flying.

Jessie spotted Fanny and ran to pick her up but Fanny growled and ran away. Jessie chased after her calling, "Here Fanny, here kitty, kitty, kitty."

"She's scared, Jessie," said her father.

Jessie pulled a chunk of kibble from the bowl and crept toward Fanny. "Here Fanny," she said in a sing-song voice. "I have some nice food for you."

Fanny stepped away.

"Let's leave her be. She'll come and eat when she wants to."

Jessie went back to Gus, dropped the food into his dish, and petted the top of his head. "Listen to Gus, Dad. He purrs and eats at the same time."

"So he does. Come on Jessie, we'll come back in the morning and check on them."

"Okay." She bent to pet Gus one last time and asked, "Do you know if Stacie is coming to get Fanny tomorrow and take her home?"

"You'll have to ask your mother about that."

"Oh," said Jessie. She took her father's hand and rested her other hand on the dog's back. "See you tomorrow," she called as they left the barn. "Good night and don't let the bed bugs bite!"

Fanny hurried out of hiding and joined Gus at the bowl. "Nice people?" she asked.

"The best," said Gus.

"You can tell me all about them later." She pushed his

head out of the way and took a mouthful of kibble.

“It’s the brown, red, and yellow kind, Fanny.”

“I know,” said Fanny purring and eating at the same time.

Chapter Seven

Purr Purr

“COCK-A-DOODLE-DO!” Ralph crowed.

“Thank you for the wake-up crow, you big red chicken. I’m up. I’m up,” said Fanny. She climbed down from the hayloft and squeezed under the barn door and found Gus sitting outside watching robins run and hop about in the lawn.

“Good morning, Master Guard Cat.”

“Good morning, Princess Fantas-ti-cat. You look great! How did you like sleeping in my historic Gitwell Barn?”

“I would have much preferred sleeping on Stacie’s soft bed, or maybe snuggled up next to Tess on the couch, but as far as sleeping in a barn goes,” she arched her back and opened her mouth into a wide yawn, “it wasn’t bad.”

“Not bad is good, right?”

“Hmmm,” said Fanny.

“Well, how would you like to take a proper tour of my domain this morning?"

"Domain?” She curtsied. “Nothing would please me

more than to tour your vast lands, your Majesty."

"Ha, ha, funny cat, come on. I have so much to show you."

Fanny felt something moving in the fur on her leg. She sat down and licked and licked at the spot. *Oh my word, I've been here so long I might have fleas!!! This can't be happening.* "Gus, do you think Tess will come for me today? I'm worried she's forgotten me."

"How could she forget you? You ARE a princess after all."

Fanny licked her paw and cleaned her face. "Princess Fantas-ti-cat!"

"Come on," Gus said. "You've seen Ralph's farm, let me show you the Gitwell Farm!"

"Okay, I'm coming."

They left the barn, crossed the driveway and padded back to a small wooden building with big windows of wire mesh and a little fenced-in yard that looked much like Ralph's. "Chicken coop and yard," said Gus. He nudged Fanny and ran a few feet to four big cages propped up in the air on tall legs. He climbed up on top of them. "Rabbit hutches," he said then hopped down and ran to a dirt pen with a shiny silver tub at

the edge. “This is a pig pen.”

“Gus, these are all empty. Where are all the animals that are suppose to live here?”

“I’m not sure, but I hope they come back.”

“Don’t worry big cat! At least when they’re gone you don’t have to worry about fresh cow-pies.”

Gus laughed. “Come on, there’s more to see.” He took her to a woodshed. They climbed on top of several neatly stacked rows of split firewood, then Gus hopped down and ran out into a field. “This used to be a huge vegetable garden. Come on, follow me. There’s more to see.”

Fanny didn’t follow him. In fact, she stopped and lay down. He kept going for a minute before he realized she wasn't behind him. He doubled back and found her sprawled out on the ground grooming. "What are you doing?"

"Sunbathing."

"Not here. I know the perfect spot." He started back toward the barn. "Follow me!"

Follow me! Come on! she thought and licked her paw to clean her face. "What is the matter with this spot right here?"

Gus padded back and looked down at the beautiful calico cat. "This spot? Right here? This is a great place to hunt or BE hunted. It's not a great place to get all comfortable and start dozing. You might just end up becoming someone's meal."

Fanny yawned.

Gus sighed. "Fanny, it's not safe to sunbathe here. Whoodeenie has probably gone to his nest to roost for the day. But you're out in the open here! The hawks and eagles are out! And don't even get me started talking about dogs or worse, coyotes! Yikes! So follow me, I'll take you to the perfect sunbathing place."

Fanny closed her eyes.

"Please," Gus said.

Fanny opened her eyes and batted them at Gus.

"This way." He took two steps, stopped, and looked back to see if Fanny was following. "My barn has a lean-to and its roof is the absolute perfect place to sunbathe."

She twitched her tail. *Sheesh!* "What is a lean-to?"

"The lean-to is the little shed that looks like it's leaning against the outside of the barn. Kind of like the barn's carport."

"You mean that part of the barn that looks like a big wing off the side?"

"Exactly," said Gus. He stood on his hind legs and held his arm straight out like a wing, then dropped it a little. "You know, I'm the barn. My head is the barn roof, and my arm is the lean-to attached to its side."

"Yeah, Gus, I've seen it," said Fanny.

Fanny followed as Gus trotted to the barn, hopped in the open window, climbed up to the hayloft, squeezed through an opening between the wall and the roof, and padded out onto the roof of the barn's lean-to. He sprawled out on his side and waited for her.

Fanny stepped out on the warm metal roof. She settled herself next to Gus and purred. "Nice."

"I told you," Gus said. "This barn is a wonderful place."

"Hmmm," Fanny purred. "I doubt a coyote could

climb up here and bother us, but what about the hawks and eagles?"

Gus pointed to the opening they had just crawled through. "If one of those big, bad birds swoops by, we hop back inside."

"Hmmm," she said. "Purr."

"I'll stand watch for danger while you nap, then you take a turn," said Gus.

"Hmmm. Purr."

After a time Gus roused Fanny. "It's your turn." He waited until she yawned and cleaned her face with her paw before he lay down and went to sleep.

Fanny watched him snoozing for several minutes and then just couldn't resist the urge to tickle him. She carefully touched the hair inside his ear. He twitched his ear. Next she touched his whiskers. He wiggled his nose. She snickered and touched it again. He wiggled his nose and batted his paw at the air by his face.

A little yellow car stopped at the back door of the old farmhouse. Gus lifted his head and looked all around.

"We've got company," said Fanny.

Chapter Eight

Giggle Giggle

All four doors of a little yellow car opened at the same time. A tall woman, a short woman, and two young girls spilled out. The girls were so much alike. They both had strawberry blonde hair tied up in pig tails. Their giggles made matching dimples in their cheeks. They both wore blue pants and red sneakers with bright pink, flopping laces. If it weren't for the fact that one of them had a little pair of round glasses sliding down her nose and the other didn't, they could have been twins. With baby dolls clutched in their arms, the girls ran, hand-in-hand, up the driveway to the barn yelling, "Gus-Gus! Fanny!"

Fanny and Gus darted off the roof and ran down the driveway. Fanny turned to Gus and yowled, "They came for me! They didn't forget me! Tess, Stacie, I'm here!"

"Look at that, Tess," Peggy said as they followed the girls up the driveway to the barn. "Gus and Fanny are friends."

Peggy swung the barn doors open and they all went inside.

"Let US feed them, Mama," Jessie said.

Gus wound round and round Peggy's legs meowing at the top of his lungs.

"How's my master guard cat?" Peggy asked. She bent down and petted him. "How's my handsome Augustus? You must be pretty hungry." She opened the lid of a wooden box and unrolled the top of a kitty kibble bag. “You feed Gus, Jessie. Then let Stacie feed Fanny."

The girls filled the bowls and Gus and Fanny made a bee line for their food. The girls squatted beside their cats and petted them while the cats ate. “My cat purrs when she eats,” Stacie said.

“Gus purrs while he’s eating too, if I pet him,” said Jessie.

“Well, Fanny purrs every time she eats,” said Stacie, pushing her glasses back up the bridge of her nose, “even if I’m not petting her.”

"You girls have fun, but stay out of trouble,” said Tess. We'll load Fanny up in her pet taxi right before we leave.”

We’ll be working down at the farmhouse if you need us,” said Peggy.

"Okay!” the girls sang out.

Gus had his fill of the kibble. He took a few steps away from the bowl and licked his mouth. Jessie picked him up and put him back in front of his bowl. "You need to eat some more," she said.

Gus took another bite of food then looked over at

Fanny. She lifted her head from her bowl, her mouth full of kibble, and snickered. Gus sighed.

Stacie stood up and brushed off her pants. "Let's play dolls." Jessie followed her outside. Gus and Fanny wandered over to a circle of sunlight on the barn floor and curled up for a catnap.

"Hey!" said Fanny.

Gus opened his eyes and saw Stacie lifting Fanny by her belly. Then he felt the air squeeze out of his lungs as Jessie snatched him up from the floor for a short jerky ride to a blanket the girls had spread out on the grass. Jessie sat down crisscross applesauce next to Stacie and settled Gus in her lap. He was just starting to really enjoy all the petting Jessie was giving him when suddenly he felt his front leg being pulled through the sleeve of a red and white checked shirt. Before he could react to that she pulled the shirt over his back and his other front leg through the other sleeve. "What are you doing?" Gus meowed. "I don't like this!"

Jessie nuzzled his head. "You are so cute, Gus-Gus." She cradled him in her arms. "Isn't he just the cutest cat?"

Stacie settled Fanny on her lap. "Gus is a boy cat. He

can't be cute," said Stacie. "He's handsome or something like that." She pulled a yellow and white poke-a-dot dress off her doll and tried to pull the dress over Fanny's head. Fanny growled and squirmed away. Stacie caught her by her tail and put her back on her lap. "Let's try that again," she said and pulled the dress over her head. Fanny growled.

Gus was not enjoying this at all. Jessie pulled his back leg into the leg hole of a pair of little, red shorts. He didn't want to scratch or bite Jessie but this was just too much. He growled and tried to get away, but Jessie had a strong hold of him. She pushed his other leg through and hiked the shorts up then pulled his tail through one of the leg holes. Gus growled louder, squirmed loose, and ran a few steps away.

Fanny tried to get away too. She growled at Stacie when she pulled her back legs through a pair of white shorts then she bit her. "Bad kitty!" Stacie cried. Fanny felt bad and stopped squirming. "That's better," said Stacie. She held her up for Jessie to see. "Isn't she the cutest cat?"

The girls scooped up the cats and carried them all around the barn. "They need to take a nap," said Stacie. The girls took the cats out to their blanket and set them down. Fanny and Gus bolted away as soon

as their feet touched the ground. They ran down the driveway toward the farmhouse and dove under a rhododendron plant.

"GIRLS, COME GIVE US A HAND!" Peggy called from the farmhouse.

The girls shouted, “Okay!” and skipped down the driveway hand-in-hand.

Chapter Nine

Ice Cream!

The girls skidded to a stop beside Peggy. She wrapped her arms around them in a big bear hug. "We need you two to help us carry this old trunk up to the barn."

Stacie walked around it and ran her hand over the curved lid and down the leather straps that wrapped over the top and buckled like one of her father's belts in front. "Hey, look at this." On the front of the trunk was a shiny brass plate with letters engraved in the center. She bent over and read, "R. X. Gitwell. What's a R. X. Gitwell?"

Peggy gave the trunk a few more swipes with a towel. "That is a name plate. This steamer trunk belonged to Jessie's," she held up her hand and counted on her fingers, "great, great, great, uncle, R. X. Gitwell. People used trunks like this in the old days when they traveled. It was their suitcase."

"This is a BIG suitcase," said Stacie.

"What's in it?" Jessie asked.

"Old clothes, knick-knacks, blankets, toiletries, things like that," said Peggy.

The girls giggled. They looked at each other and said, "Toiletries?"

Tess ruffled the girls' hair. "Toiletries are things like soaps, lotions, cologne, and hairbrushes. Things like that."

Still laughing, Stacie asked, "Can we see inside?"

"It's locked and I didn't bring the key," said Peggy.

"Aah!" the girls said.

"We need your strong muscles to help us move this to the barn." Peggy squeezed Jessie's and Stacie's skinny arms. "There's a leather handle on each end of the trunk. Jessie, you help me lift with this handle and Stacie, you help your mother with that one. Ready?"

Gus and Fanny hid under the rhododendron plant. Fanny bit and yanked at the bottom of the skirt Stacie had dressed her in, but all it did was pull her neck down. Gus had an itch on his shoulder. He scratched at it with his hind paw and his claw stuck in the fabric of the shirt Jessie had dressed him in. He tugged and tugged and finally got his claw free. They watched as Peggy, Tess, Jessie, and Stacie hauled the trunk up the driveway. "I know what that is," said Gus.

Fanny stopped biting at her dress. "What is it?"

"That's Hilma's trunk."

"Hilma?" asked Fanny.

Gus ran ahead. "Yessiree Bob! And Hilma is not going to be happy about them taking her trunk out of the house."

“Who is Hilma? Gus! Who is Hilma?” Fanny called.

“I’ll tell you later. Come on!”

Fanny stumbled over the dress, but managed to run behind Gus from bush to bush, tree to tree, staying out of sight as they followed the trunk up the driveway.

The troop of women and girls were halfway to the barn when Peggy said, "Let's set it down for a minute. How’s everyone doing?"

Fanny peeked around a large fir tree at the steamer

trunk and asked again, "Who is Hilma?"

"Shhhhh!" said Gus.

"Did you just shush me?" Fanny asked. "Don't shush me!"

Gus sighed. "I'll tell you later."

Meanwhile, Stacie and Jessie were panting. "It's heavy," said Jessie.

"Not much farther now," said Tess. She wiped her brow with the back of her hand. "Tell us when you're ready to go again."

Stacie hopped up on the trunk and sat down. "I wonder where this thing has been. Do you suppose it was on a ship in the ocean? Maybe it was on the Titanic!"

"It would be at the bottom of the ocean if it were on the Titanic!" said Jessie. "The Titanic sunk."

"Your father tells me that Doctor R. X. Gitwell and his wife did a lot of traveling back and forth to her home country in Europe. So, I think this trunk just might have been on a sea voyage or two," said Peggy.

Stacie pretended to paddle the trunk and then she hopped down and grabbed the handle. The four of them carried the trunk the rest of the way to the barn. Gus and Fanny followed. Gus hopped through the barn window. Fanny stumbled when her paw caught on the skirt of the dress. She righted herself, shook her head, and this time was able to jump through the window, too. Once in the barn the cats hid under the tractor.

Peggy and Tess shoved the trunk against the wall. "Thank you, girls," Peggy said.

"I think that deserves an ice cream cone from the Dari Delish!" Tess sang out.

Jessie and Stacie jumped up and down and shouted, "Yes!"

"I have a few more things to finish up at the farmhouse and then we'll go," said Peggy.

The cats hid from the girls and watched them pick up their dolls and the blanket. Peggy brought a wheelbarrow full of boxes and stacked them in the empty stanchion where Betty, the cow, used to be milked and closed the barn door.

"Stacie!" Tess called. "Put Fanny in her carrier so we can take her home."

HOME! Fanny thought. She glanced over at Gus. He was looking at her with a dopey sad face. *Ah, he looks sad to see me leave. Too bad, because I'm going HOME!*

I'm finally going home.

The girls tiptoed all around the barnyard calling, "Here, Fanny. Here kitty, kitty, kitty!"

Gus hung his head and whispered, "Are you going to go with Stacie now? I have so much more to show you." He nudged Fanny's shoulder.

"Sorry, Gus, but I really want to go home." Fanny crouched down to crawl under the barn door, but her paw caught on the skirt and she stumbled. She stood up and tried again. This time the skirt caught on the barn door. She yanked and yanked on it and finally freed herself. But it was too late.

Peggy and Tess were in the little yellow car. Tess called, " Let's go, girls! I've left the pet taxi on the picnic table. We'll come back for Fanny later! I'm starving!"

The girls ran to the car yelling, "Yay! You scream, I scream, we all scream for ice cream!" Once in the car Stacie yelled out the window, "We'll be back, Fanny!"

Fanny ran down the driveway and stopped at the picnic table. Gus came and sat beside her. She bit and tugged at the poke-a-dot dress and uttered a quiet menacing growl.

Chapter Ten

Cackle Cackle

Gus nudged Fanny. “Don’t worry, Fanny. See, they left your pet taxi there on the picnic table.”

“But what does that mean, Gus?”

“It means they’ll be back for you! Come on back to the barn. I think a little catnap will make you feel better.”

Fanny hung her head and trudged back to the barn. Gus trotted happily behind her.

Meanwhile, Hilma and her loyal companion, Kit Kat materialized out of the steamer trunk and sat on the lid. "I haven't been in this barn in ages!" she said.

She pulled Kit Kat onto her lap, stroked the cat's fur, and surveyed the area. She threw her head back, laughed, cackled, and shouted, "GUS!" when she saw the cats crawl under the barn door.

Gus growled. "What's so funny?"

Fanny froze and crouched to the floor.

Hilma flew over the cats. She reached out with her cold ghostly hand and patted Fanny's head. Fanny yowled a high pitched, loud yow like she'd never yowled in her life.

"Hey, Hilma," said Gus.

Hilma flew over them again and touched each cat by the ear. Fanny hissed, "Who or what is Hilma?"

Hilma patted Gus's head. "Do tell, Gus. Tell this calico minx about me."

"Fanny, Hilma is a human ghost that lived in the farmhouse a long, long time ago."

"Not just lived in the farmhouse, Gus!," said Hilma. "We brought life into that house!"

Gus sat down in front of Fanny. He glanced at Hilma who was sitting on the trunk tapping her long fingernail on her front tooth. "Go on," she coaxed.

"The farmhouse used to be the jewel of the county when Hilma LIVED there. It was painted a bright white with blue shutters. There were beautiful flower beds that surrounded the big front porch and a huge vegetable garden that filled the kitchens of many houses in the county with fresh produce. Every holiday Hilma and her husband the doctor moved furniture out of the front room and held dances. The doctor brought a Victrola back from one of his voyages and all the latest music filled the house. But Hilma preferred live music so, more often than not, a band of locals played and sang. Doctor Gitwell's medical office was in one of the downstairs bedrooms. He called Hilma his Nurse Nightingale. Together they made people well again." He turned to Hilma. "Better?"

"Ah, there is so much more, but that's better, Gus. Much better," said Hilma.

Kit Kat swirled around the barn then came to a stop in front of Fanny. "Boo," she said.

Fanny arched her back, hissed, and spat.

"Come here, my precious," Hilma called to Kit Kat. "I don't think Miss Fanny likes us." Kit Kat drifted to

Hilma and sat on her lap and purred.

“That was Kit Kat, Hilma’s ghost Siamese cat. She’s Hilma’s loyal companion and she lived all her nine lives on the farm with Hilma,” said Gus.

Fanny looked all around. “You can see them? Why can’t I see them?”

“I don’t know,” said Gus.

“Oh, for heaven’s sake! I’m right here, Fanny!”

Fanny gaped at Hilma and Kit Kat as they slowly materialized. First, just Hilma’s head floated in the air above the steamer trunk. She smiled and in a very low moan said, “Hello, Fanny.” Then the rest of her body and all of Kit Kat materialized.

Fanny crouched down and inched closer to Gus.

"So, here we are, Gus," said Hilma. "You, me, Kit Kat, and your little friend," Hilma flew over the cats and touched Fanny's tail, "in the barn."

Fanny pulled her tail tight around herself.

"And, I see you've let the little girls dress you up like clowns. Seriously, Gus! You two look pretty silly."

Fingers came through the barn window and landed on the wooden floor with a thud. He shook his head. "Hey, cat. I'm here for my cut," he said.

R.X. Gitwell

Gus stared at the raccoon, but didn't move.

"Kitty kibble, Gus! Now!" said Fingers. He waddled over and tugged on the red checked shirt hanging from Gus's shoulders. "Nice duds," he snickered.

Hilma flew back to her trunk. She sat on the lid, crossed her legs, and swung her foot. "Kit Kat!" she called. Kit Kat drifted to her and curled up on her lap.

Fingers waddled a few steps toward Hilma's trunk. "Hey Hilma," said Fingers. "Hey, Kit Kat, I neva expected to see youz twos here!"

Hilma tossed her head and cackled. She and Kit Kat swooped around Fanny, then flew back to the steamer trunk and seeped back inside. Hilma's eerie voice floated out of the trunk. "It was nice to meet you, Miss Fanny. I hope we'll be friends."

The fur on Fanny's back stood on end and she shivered. She turned toward the trunk and replied. "The pleasure is all mine? I'm sure? I think?"

"Manners, Kit Kat, the calico princess has manners," said Hilma cackling and laughing. "Yes, indeed, Miss Fanny. The pleasure is all yours. Ha, ha, ha!"

Fingers padded over to Fanny and tugged on her poke-a-dot dress, and then he poked Gus in the shoulder. "Gus! Kibble! Now! I ain't got all day." He circled around the pair of cats and laughed so hard that he got the hiccups. "Youz need my expertise gettin' out of them fine threads youz wearin?"

"Yes!" said Fanny. "Please." Fingers pulled the little dress over Fanny's head.

Gus stood up. "Get the kibble yourself!" He jumped up into the hayloft. "Come on, Fanny!" He squeezed under the opening to the lean-to roof. His shirt snagged on the wood and was ripped off.

"OOOWEEEEOOO!" Hilma called from the trunk.

Fanny hurried to join Gus. He had torn the little shorts off that he was wearing and Fanny did the same. "Hilma and Kit Kat are creepy!"

Gus laid down and put his head on his paws. "They aren't so bad."

"I can hear you!" Hilma cackled. "Ha ha ha ha ha!"

"Creepy," Fanny whispered. "Where is Dr. Gitwell? Is he a ghost, too?"

"No one knows," said Gus.

Chapter Eleven

Hop Hop

Once or twice, every day, Gus followed Fanny to the pet taxi still sitting on the picnic table. She'd climb on its top and ask, "Why isn't Tess coming to get me? Why isn't she taking me home?"

"Don't worry, she'll come for you. But even if she doesn't, you're always welcome here."

"That's nice of you to say, Gus."

On the fifth day Fanny went to the picnic table, but didn't jump to the top of the pet taxi. "They aren't going to take me home. They are never going to take me home." She cried a yowing cat cry.

Gus sat down next to her and nudged her shoulder. "I know you want to go home, but this is so cool! Really, it is! There's still so much to show you around here. I'm glad you're still here! They'll come for you. Don't you worry about that."

"Ah, Gus-Gus." Fanny purred and rubbed Gus shoulder to shoulder. "You have been very kind."

Fanny got used to the routine in the barn. She woke to the sound of Ralph's crow every morning just as the sun was coming up. Then, moments after that, just like clockwork, Fingers barged into the barn shouting, "Hey! Cats! I'm here for the protection chow youz owe me!" He'd stand up and strut around the barn floor on his back legs pounding on his chest. "I'm here for my cut, cats!" Then he'd chomp up the food they left for him, lick his lips, clean and shine his pinky ring, and leave. The ghosts, Hilma and Kit Kat, were eerily quiet most of the time. Except that every evening, just as the sun was setting, they would seep out of the trunk and fly around inside the barn three times moaning and yowling and then seep back into their steamer truck.

On the fifth night in the barn, Fanny watched Marvin and Marcia, Gus's mice friends, scuttle past her and stop. She turned to Gus and said, "Are you going to let those mice stay in here with you?"

"Fanny! Really? You know I owe my life to those two little mice. If Marvin and Marcia hadn't gnawed through the net in the garden that horrible night and the coyotes had got me, I wouldn't be here today. I would have lost at least one of my nine lives that night. And you! Really! If they hadn't gnawed through the yarn of that afghan the night of the storm . . ."

"I know, I know. They saved one of my lives, too.

They're your friends. I appreciate everything they've done for me and you. Really, I do. It's just that I might forget about all that and pounce on them without even thinking. They ARE mice, after all. It's kind of an instinct, Gus. It might be best to have them live somewhere else."

Gus stared at Fanny and then, in a no nonsense voice, said, "No!"

Fanny padded to the side of the barn, stretched up, and scratched the wall with her claws. She sat down, licked her paws, and said, "It's your barn, Gus, so I'll try to remember Marvin and Marcia are your special mice friends."

"Thank you."

Fanny winked at Gus. "You're welcome!"

From high in the barn rafters, the mice watched the cats. Finally, Marcia squeaked and said, "We'd

better stay clear of that Fanny cat."

Marvin nodded his head up and down. "I agree, Marcia." The two mice scampered across the rafters and down the wall to the barn floor.

On the sixth day Fanny didn't want to follow Gus on the rounds of his domain or visit the picnic table and her pet taxi. She laid down on the warm metal roof of the lean-to and napped. "This is nice," she purred.

Gus plopped down beside her. He licked his paw and cleaned his face, then snuggled up against her. "This IS nice." He purred.

Later, Fanny took Gus out in some tall, dry grass to teach him the art of catching grasshoppers. "The key is," she told him, "to pounce and swat. Hold the hoppers down with just enough of them sticking out," she crouched down, sprung, and nailed a grasshopper to the ground, "that you're able to get them in your mouth!" She lifted her paw ever so slightly and quickly snatched the grasshopper into her mouth. She turned toward Gus, grinned exposing the little bug legs that stuck between her teeth, crunched, and swallowed her prize. "Just like that!"

"Impressive!" said Gus.

"Tastes like lemon," said Fanny.

Fanny caught sight of another grasshopper landing in the grass just to her right. She crouched and sprang catching the insect in midair.

“You know, Fanny, I’ve caught grasshoppers before, but you make it so much more fun!”

Fanny laughed. “You’ve never had a friend like me before.”

Gus watched Fanny stealthily move through the grass. *You’re right, Fanny, I’ve never had a friend quite like you.*

Both cats were so focused on hunting grasshoppers that they didn't notice two cars pull up and park at the back of the farmhouse. Fanny was ready to pounce when she heard a familiar voice calling her name.

"Fanny! Here, Fanny, here kitty, kitty, kitty," Tess called.

"TESS!" Fanny yowled, then bolted to her mistress. Gus followed close behind.

Tess scooped Fanny up and walked to the picnic table. “Are you ready to go home, Princess?”

Gus wound round Peggy's legs until she picked him up, nuzzled his furry head, and said, "We're going to miss Fanny, aren’t we?”

Gus watched Tess put Fanny in the pet taxi and then load it into her car. Fanny let out a yow and said, “Tuna fish!” She ate a bite, then looked out between the bars and said, "See ya later, Gus.” Tess closed the door, got in and drove the car away.

"Bye, Fanny," said Gus. “See ya later.”

Peggy put Gus down. He sat there in the driveway, alert, his head up, watching the car with Fanny inside disappear. He sat like that for five minutes. Finally, he scratch at a bothersome flea, shook his head, and trotted back to the barn.

Chapter Twelve

Sniff Sniff

"*Home!*" Fanny thought when Tess stopped the car in their driveway. "*Home!*" she thought again when Tess opened her pet taxi and she hopped to the ground. She padded to her box on the front porch with the pink blanket, then to her box on the patio with the green rug, then to her cushion high up on the sailboat where she could see forever, and last, her smooth warm rock next to the pond that was still filled with bright, orange fish. She stretched out on the rock and purred. "*Home.*"

The long summer days passed as slowly as restaurant ketchup from a glass bottle. Day after day, night after night, Fanny did the same thing. Three times a day she slipped into the kitchen for a tidbit of whatever Tess was cooking. She'd wind around and around Tess's legs until Tess noticed her.

"Fanny! You're going to trip me, you naughty kitty," said Tess. "Here, have a taste."

Almost every evening Stacie's dad, Jack, either played the piano or strummed his guitar. "This song is for you, Fanny," he'd say. Fanny liked to reward Jack by purring loudly and adding a yowl every now and then.

And, of course, there was little Stacie. Stacie petted, brushed, carried, and sang to Fanny. Fanny rewarded Stacie by not biting or scratching her and she allowed Stacie to cuddle her every night when she went to bed. Fanny should have been delighted, but something was missing.

One morning, while napping on the deck, Fanny heard the backdoor opening and Tess humming. There was a rattle of paper and the plink, plink, plink of kitty kibble hitting her silver bowl. "Here, Fanny. Here kitty, kitty, kitty," Tess called. Then Fanny heard the sound of the backdoor closing. Fanny looked down between the slats of the deck floor and saw a plump neighbor cat boldly walk up to her bowl and take a healthy mouthful. She jumped from the deck to the porch and scrambled after the thief. "That's mine!" she yowled. The startled, food-snatching cat tore out across the yard, under a fence, and straight down the sidewalk with Fanny hot on its tail. Neighborhood dogs barked from behind windows or strained at tethers in front lawns as they shot past. When Fanny finally stopped chasing she yelled, "And don't come back!" She took a moment to lick her paw and clean her face and then, head held high, she pranced back home. *Look at me, Gus. Now I'm a Master Guard Cat, too,* she thought. But Gus wasn't there.

Life was quiet at Fanny's house. She used to love to curl up on her rug on the patio, her head lolling back and forth, watching big ships move up and down the Columbia River or ospreys or eagles swooping over the water before splashing down to catch a fish. She used to be content to spend long hours simply laying on her blanket on the front porch and watching, through half opened eyes, the cars, people, and dogs on leashes passing by. But now these things bored her. She missed the excitement of the Gitwell Farm.

She tired of chasing scolding squirrels up the trees. It just wasn't fun playing by herself. Fanny missed her best friend. Fanny missed Gus.

Meanwhile, back on the farm Gus was enjoying himself. Ralph's crow woke him every morning and the sound of frogs croaking and crickets chirping lulled him to sleep every night. He even made a new friend, a golden deer. He saw her one afternoon under the apple tree and stalked her all the way across the garden. When he got close she raised her

head and said, "Hi! My name is Darla." They started chatting and found they had something in common. They were both very afraid of coyotes. Gus's life was almost back to normal on the farm, but something was missing. He missed having someone to share everything with. He missed having a best friend. He missed Fanny.

Then, one hot day at the tail end of summer, Fanny found herself back in the pet taxi staring at a little bowl of tuna fish.

Stacie poked her fingers through the bars of the pet taxi, petted Fanny's side, and said,"It's not your fault you have to leave, Fanny. It's just that Great Aunt Stephanie has a really, really, REALLY bad allergy to cats. Not just to you." Fanny ate the tuna and licked the bowl clean.

Tess carried the pet taxi with Fanny in it to her car and set it on the backseat. Stacie climbed in alongside it, put her face up to the bars, and said, "Auntie Stephanie broke her hip bone." She pointed to her own hip bone, "This one right here, when she was climbing down the steps of Dad's travel trailer. Dad says she has to stay at our house with us until she's good to go." Stacie's eyes filled with tears. "So, Mom says you have to go until Auntie Stephanie is better."

Tess got in the car and started the motor. "Buckle up, Stacie."

Stacie buckled her seatbelt and Fanny paced inside the pet taxi. Stacie whispered to Fanny, "I love my Great Auntie, I do. And I don't want her to sneeze

her head off. But I'm going to really miss you, Fanny." She wiped her nose with the back of her hand. Fanny laid down. "I'll come see you everyday to be sure you have lots of food to eat." Stacie opened the cage door and put her hand inside. Fanny purred when Stacie petted her.

The car stopped and Tess climbed out. Stacie scooped Fanny out of the pet taxi and squeezed her. Tess opened Stacie's door. Stacie kissed the top of Fanny's head then put her down on the ground. Fanny looked all around and exclaimed, "The Farm! The Farm?"

Gus was napping on the barn roof when he heard the unmistakable sound of Fanny's yowl. He ran down the driveway toward Tess's car but came to a screeching halt a few feet away from her. Fanny meowed quietly. Stacie gave her cat a pat on the head. Fanny purred and wrapped around the little girl's legs, then walked over to Gus. "Hi!" The cats touched noses.

"We've got to be going now, Stacie," said Tess. "Fanny will be just fine."

Stacie took her mother's hand and slowly climbed back into the car. She rolled down the window and

called, "Bye, Fanny." She sniffled. "Be a good kitty."

Fanny and Gus turned to head back to the barn. "Nice skid marks, Gus," Fanny said admiring the marks Gus made in the gravel when he skidded to a stop earlier. "Did you miss me?"

Whoodeenie silently swooped overhead. Both cats ducked and ran to the barn.

Chapter Thirteen

Boooooooo Whoooooooo

Summer ended, autumn flew past like leaves whistling in the wind, and winter arrived on the Gitwell Farm.

"The first puff and youz outta here!" said Fingers.

Bud lifted his head. "I can stay?" he asked.

"You can stay," said Gus.

Bud skipped in a circle around and around the barn floor, his black and white tail waving behind him like a furry flag. "I can stay, I can stay, I can stay," he sang. He hurried under the barn and stirred up a small dust storm digging out a little nest for himself there. He slept a lot that winter. And even though he never puffed, there was always a faint skunk smell coming from his corner of the barn .

As much as Fanny didn't like to admit it, she kind of liked having Fingers stay in the barn too. He made a cozy spot for himself among the boxes Peggy moved to the barn from the farmhouse. He pushed them around just enough to make a trail back to a cozy, little area he lined with loose straw. "I have lotsa duties, lotsa responsibilities, bein' that I'm second in command of Tony's gang and all," he told Gus. "There's more than youz knows goes inta keepin all youz neighborhood pets safe!" Every so often, Fingers would slip out during the night. But, most of the winter, you could find him sleeping in his nest in the barn too.

At first, Paul refused to stay in the barn with Bud. "I'm a 'possum; I can't live in the same barn as a skunk! Since Bud is staying in here, I'm not!" He made his nest in a pile of rocks next to the driveway. He would have stayed there all winter, too, but he gave it up and moved into the barn after the first heavy rain. "I don't want to spend the whole winter wet," was all he said. He moved some of the boxes around to make a nest near Fingers, but Hilma was forever seeping out of her trunk and scaring him into fainting.

“Why youz gotta do that to poor Pauly?” Fingers asked her.

“What? I'm a ghost. That's what ghosts do,” Hilma replied.

Paul finally settled under the barn as far from Bud and Hilma as he could manage.

Hilma spent most of her time shut up in her steamer

trunk, sometimes quietly crying and moaning.

"Why do you suppose Hilma cries so much?" Fanny asked Gus.

"She says it's because when she was still alive and living in the farmhouse her Dr. Gitwell left on a sea voyage and never came back. She's been mourning him ever since."

"That's just too sad," said Fanny. "She must have really liked him!"

Late one afternoon Marvin and Marcia saw Fanny catch and dispatch a plump brown field mouse to mouse heaven. It happened so fast it made their little heads spin.

Twitchy-nose to twitchy-nose, Marvin said, "Gus made Fanny promise to not harm us."

"I know, but she's a cat. We are mice," said Marcia. "I think it would be a good idea to move our nest farther away from her."

"I agree. I would rather be safe than sorry," said Marvin.

They scouted every inch of the barn, but no place was right. Then they jumped down to the soft dry dirt under the barn. Marvin saw it first and pointed to the perfect place, a stack of old tires. Marcia squeaked and scurried past him and started digging. In no time, they built a burrow below the tires and went about stocking their new home with a large cache of seeds for the winter.

The animals in Gus's barn were ready for winter. Everyone except Fanny, that is. She glanced at Gus sprawled out on top of a bale of hay. *Tess and Stacie visit me pretty often, but they never bring my pet taxi. Jack comes with his guitar and plays and sings to me, but he doesn't bring the pet taxi, either. Is the Farm my home now? I feel so unsettled. I still love Tess, Stacie, and Jack, but I love it here on the farm with Gus more.* She batted Gus's ear. He raised his head and then rolled on his back and batted her back. She sighed and settled herself next to him. Gus laid on his back, gravity pulling his lips back into a quirky cat smile, and purred.

Chapter Fourteen

La De Da La De Da

One cold, dark, winter morning Fingers came back into the barn and, while waddling back to his nest, knocked over one of Peggy's cardboard boxes, dumping everything out on the floor. He grumbled as he righted the box and started jamming everything back inside. Hilma heard the commotion and seeped out of her trunk to see what was going on. She rolled her eyes at the clumsy raccoon, but then she looked more closely at the things strewn on the floor. They were her things. When she saw Fingers pick up a red scarf, she grabbed hold of it, and gave it a tug. He tugged back. Hilma tugged harder.

Everyone in the barn watched the tug of war. Gus's jaw dropped and his eyes opened wide. Fanny ducked down and pulled her tail over her face. Bud tried to hide under the tractor. Paul dropped like a rock to the barn floor. Marvin and Marcia scurried nervously back and forth under the barn looking up between the slats of the barn floor.

Hilma shouted, “Give it to me!”

Fingers shouted, “No!”

“GIVE IT TO ME!” Hilma shouted louder.

The tug of war ended when Fingers said, “Fine,” and let go. Hilma snatched the scarf from Fingers, flew up into the hayloft, and wound it around her neck.

Gus let out a high-pitched, nervous cat scream, "Hilma! I didn't know you could do that!"

"What?" Hilma asked looking at each of them.

"Your hands! You’re using your hands! You're a ghost, Hilma!"

Hilma threw her head back and cackled. "So I am, Gus." She tied and untied the scarf. "This was a gift from my dear husband, Dr. R. X. Gitwell, on our first Valentine's Day together as man and wife.”

"But, Hilma, you said you weren't strong enough to . . . to . . . to . . .," Gus stammered.

"Not strong enough to grasp objects? Is that what you are trying to ask?" said Hilma. "Isn't it grand? I'm getting stronger. It must be this barn!"

Hilma flew to Gus, the scarf trailing behind her. She dangled the scarf in front of him. He couldn't resist and reached to bat at it, but stopped and pulled his paw away as though the scarf were burning hot.

Hilma cackled again and wound the scarf around her neck.

Fingers stood on his hind legs and said,"I don't knowz what youz guys are so worked up about. Hilma's just a little touchy about her old scarf."

Gus rolled his eyes. Fanny pulled her tail tighter around herself. Marvin and Marcia disappeared into their burrow. Paul didn't even twitch. And Bud shivered.

Hilma started singing, "Let me call you sweetheart, you belong to me, la de da, la de da," and seeped back into her steamer trunk tugging the red scarf through the crack in the lid inside with her.

Fingers nudged Paul with his toe. He turned to Gus

and said, “That Hilma, she’s a might touchy about her things. A might touchy, ha, ha, get it?”

Gus shook his head and then he and Fanny jumped up into the hayloft. Bud joined Fingers.

“A might touchy!” Fingers said again laughing.

“I CAN HEAR YOU!” Hilma shouted from inside her trunk.

Fingers shrugged and rolled Paul over. “Rise and shine, ole buddy.”

Paul blinked several times, then slowly got up.

“You missed all the excitement,” said Bud.

So, winter settled over the Gitwell Farm. Hilma practiced picking up objects in the barn, cackling happily when she was successful and shrieking grumpily when she wasn’t. Rob tacked a blue tarp over the hole in barn’s roof keeping the rain, snow and, best of all, Whoodeenie out. Fingers, Paul, Bud, and even Marvin and Marcia slept a lot. Gus and Fanny ventured out most everyday to patrol the territory.

Stacie came to the farm with Jessie as often as she could. One gray rainy day Stacie stormed into the barn and scooped Fanny up in her arms and nuzzled her face into Fanny's soft fur and sobbed, "It's going to be a long, long time until I can take you home. Great Auntie Stephanie is not getting better very fast. I think she might live with us forever."

Stacie was sad and Fanny felt sorry for her. So, she did the only thing she could. She purred.

After Stacie and Jessie left, Gus asked Fanny, "Are you happy here?"

Fanny licked her paw and cleaned her face. "Are you happy I'm here?"

Gus touched Fanny nose to nose and said, "I am and I hope you stay here forever."

"Me too, Gus. Me too!" Fanny purred.

Chapter Fifteen

Achooo Achooo!

Gus woke because of a tickle in his nose. He tried to go back to sleep, but now, his nose not only tickled, it was running. He wiped it with his paw. He might have fallen back to sleep, but Ralph crowed.

"Ah, I might as well . . . AAACHOOO!" He sneezed a sneeze that made his head twist and snot fly. "I might as well . . . AAACHOOO . . . get up."

Fanny nudged him away and covered her face with her luxurious tail. "Bless you."

"Thank you." He stretched and walked to the edge of the hayloft. "I think I'll go out and patrol the area. Would you like to come with me?"

Fanny stirred, lifted her head, and looked at her friend. "A girl needs her beauty sleep."

"You're already beautiful," said Gus, "to me."

Fanny shook her head. "Go, Master Guard Cat." Fanny laid her face back down and purred.

Gus was greeted by the golden glow of the sun slowly rising in the east. *BEAUTIFUL!* he thought. He sat down and watched it slowly ascending the horizon, then he got up and crossed the driveway, skirted around a big brown mud puddle, and walked out in the soft green grass of the hayfield. He watched a robin fly up and disappear into the white blossoms of an apple tree. "AAACHOOO!" He trotted over to an old claw foot bathtub full of water, hopped up on the rim, and lapped up a cold drink. He watched a bumble bee flying in and out of a sea of yellow flowers along the fence. His nose started to run, then tickle.

"AAACHOOO!" He tumbled off the side of the tub, but still managed to land on his feet. He licked his paw and cleaned his face. As he slowly put his paw back on the ground he exclaimed, "Eureka! Ah ha! I know what this is! The flowers are blooming! The grass is growing! The birds are singing! I'm sneezing and my nose is running! This happens once a year! IT'S SPRING!" He did a little dance and sang, "SPRING IS HERE!"

"Hey there Gus, ole friend, what are youz goin' on about?" Fingers asked.

Gus snapped his head around and saw Fingers waddling out from under the barn door. "Springtime, seed-time, flowering, budding, sing-time, that's what's going on, Fingers! Can't you feel it?"

"Now that youz mention it, it does feel just a tad

springy." Fingers danced in a circle. Gus joined him. They hummed and pranced in the grass until Fingers stopped abruptly and Gus slammed into him. Fingers growled and looked into the flowers. Gus followed his gaze. There stood a smaller version of Fingers, a prettier version of Fingers, a fluffy lady raccoon.

"Hi," she said.

Gus said hello and waited for Fingers to say hello, too, but he didn't. Fingers stood there staring at the lady raccoon with his mouth wide open not saying a word. Gus reached up and closed his friend's mouth.

The pretty raccoon batted her eyes at Fingers and said, "I think I'm lost. My name is Ramona."

Gus nudged Fingers, but he just stood there gawking at Ramona, so finally he said, "I'm Gus, this is Fingers, and you're on the Gitwell Farm." Fingers remained silent so, Gus continued, "Where did you come from?"

"I came from over there." She pointed. "I live at the fairgrounds. I feel so silly. I was out enjoying the sunshine when a dog caught me daydreaming and chased me. I'm afraid I panicked and ran and now I don't know the way back." She batted her eyes at Fingers again. "Could you help me find my way back home?"

Fingers was speechless and stood still as a statue. No amount of poking from Gus made him talk, so once again he spoke for his friend. "Well, you have to go to the end of the garden, cross the road, and . . ."

Fingers shouted, "RRRRRRRRamona!" The r's rolling off his tongue.

Both Gus and Ramona jumped straight up in the air, startled by Fingers' outburst. Ramona ducked into the flowers along the fence line. Gus's eyes got huge and the hair on his back stood up Mohawk style.

It took a second for Gus's heart to stop racing and then he turned to Fingers and said, "Fingers, buddy, what is the matter with you?"

"RRRRRRRRamona!" Fingers shouted again.

Gus was dumbstruck for several seconds. He'd never seen Fingers act this way before. "Yes, Fingers, she said her name is Ramona. Can you show her how to get back to the fairgrounds, or do you want me to?" Then he whispered in his ear. "Pal, you're scaring her."

Fingers tipped his head to the side and stared in-between the flowers at the pretty raccoon who was trying to slink away. Gus stepped in front of Fingers and said, "I don't know what is wrong with Fingers.

He's a nice raccoon and most of the time he's perfectly normal. It's okay to come out, he won't hurt you."

Ramona waddled out of the flowers, sat down, and ran her hands through the fur on her face. She tossed her head and batted her eyes at the both of them.

Handzie startled them all when he rounded the barn and called out, "Fingers! Tony sent me to get you. He says there's a situation you need to take care of."

Fingers instantly snapped out of his stupor. He stood on his hind legs at attention and, without taking his eyes away from Ramona said, "Youz can tell Tony I'll seez him afta I help RRRRRRRamona get back home. Right this way, little lady."

Ramona backed away and looked from raccoon to raccoon to cat and back nervously.

Fingers took a step toward her, offered his arm, and said, "Oh, I'm sorry. Did it hurt?"

Ramona took a step back, but gazed up at Fingers and said, "What?"

"It musta hurt when youz fell from heaven."

Ramona giggled. She looked at Gus. Gus shrugged his shoulders. Fingers offered his arm again and this time she took it. They took a few steps then got down on all four legs and toddled off toward the fairgrounds.

"What is the matter with Fingers?" Handzie asked Gus.

"It's spring, Handzie. It's just spring."

Chapter Sixteen

Buzz Buzz Tweet Tweet

Gus ran all the way to Ralph's farm. He skidded to a stop at the chicken yard and paced back and forth.

Ralph strutted to the fence and said, "You're here early today,"

"Its spring, old friend," Gus said breathlessly. "I feel like seizing the day! I feel like jumping for joy! I ran over here to tell you hello and have a nice day!" He turned and started back toward the Gitwell farm.

"Thank you," Ralph yelled and pecked the ground, but then he raised his head and shouted, "What does it mean to seize the day?"

"Make the most of it, Ralph," Gus called over his shoulder.

When Gus got back to the farm he went to the barn looking for Fanny. He found her sunbathing on the warm metal roof of the lean-to.

"Shhh," she said when he padded up beside her. "Be quiet. Look over there."

Out in the hayfield, noses deep down in the ground, tails in the air, dirt flying out behind them, were two skunks.

"It's our Monsieur Bouquet and he has a friend. What do you suppose they are doing?"

Gus watched the skunks for a few seconds. "They're digging up a bees' nest. See the bees swarming around them."

"Sheesh!" said Fanny. "I thought only bears did that."

"AAACHOOO!" Gus sneezed.

Both skunk heads flew out of the hole.

Gus wiped his nose and stared at the new skunk. "Ah, she's almost as cute as Bud."

"Cuter!" said Fanny.

Bud squinted up at the cats and said, "Is that you, Gus?"

The other skunk didn't hesitate; she just ran straight toward the barn in full attack mode.

"Whoa, Bud, it's me. Tell her I'm a good guy," said Gus as he jumped from the roof to greet her.

The skunk stopped just short of running right into him. She stomped her feet, hissed, and squealed. Bud hurried to her side. "It's okay, Petal, Gus is not a threat. He's my friend."

Fanny leapt off the roof and joined Gus. Petal

bristled, stomped her foot again, and started raising her tail. Bud whispered in her ear, "Friends," and gently pulled her tail down.

"Who have we got here?" Gus asked.

Bud took Petal's paw in his own and said, "Gus, Fanny, this is Petal." Petal's eyes darted back and forth at the two cats. "Petal, I'd like to introduce you to Gus and Fanny. Gus is the Master Guard Cat of this farm and Fanny is . . .," Bud stared at Fanny for a moment and then continued, "Fanny is some kind of princess. Isn't that right, Gus?"

"Yes she is." Gus gazed at Fanny. "Yes she is." Then he turned his attention back to Petal and said, "Hello, Petal."

Fanny stood up and walked in a circle around the skunks then came back and sat beside Gus. "Hmmm, where did you come from Miss Petal? Where did you meet our Bud?"

Petal and Bud started talking at the same time then stopped and looked at one another. "You can tell them," said Bud.

"Oh, no, I interrupted you. You go ahead, Bud," said Petal.

"Oh, for heaven's sake!" Hilma's loud screech shot from inside the barn. Gus and Fanny jumped. Petal and Bud trembled and threw their arms around each other. **Budkins met Petal when she came snooping around the barn! She was trespassing! Monsieur Bouquet didn't chase her away. They have been playing since the wee hours of the night. I think he is smitten! I think he is twitter-pated!"**

Gus glanced at the barn and saw Hilma float away from the window and disappear. He shook his head, turned back to Bud, and said, "Hilma says your new friend was a trespasser?"

"Well, technically, she was trespassing. I didn't invite her to come in the barn," said Bud.

"Well, she can't come in the barn anymore," said Fanny. "This time for sure, love stinks!"

Bud and Petal dropped their heads and looked at the ground.

"Fanny is right, Bud. One skunk accidentally puffing is bad enough. Two skunks accidentally puffing would be too much," said Gus.

"It's okay, Buddly. I understand," said Petal. Bud and Petal started walking away.

Gus glanced at Fanny then chased after the skunks. "Petal, wait," he said. "Just because you aren't welcome **inside** the barn doesn't mean you can't hang out together **outside** the barn."

"And, you have to PROMISE no unnecessary, accidental puffing!" said Fanny.

Bud jumped up and down. "I promise, I promise, I promise!" he said.

"Way away from the barn," said Fanny.

Petal dipped her head then shook it up and down. "I promise."

"I guess that would be okay," said Fanny.

Bud and Petal smacked their lips, touched noses, and then scampered back to their hole in the ground and were soon busy digging again.

"Twitter-pated?" Fanny asked.

Gus came back and touched Fanny nose-to-nose. "Don't ask me what Hilma means. She's a ghost. Ghosts talk weird."

"I CAN HEAR YOU, GUS," Hilma huffed. **"Twitter-pated, the whole bunch of you!"**

Gus and Fanny ran toward the garden. "I need to tell you about Ramona," said Gus.

"What is a Ramona?"

Hilma's cackle floated from the barn. **"RRRRRRRRamona! Ha, ha, ha! Let me tell you about the birds and the bees and the flowers and the trees and the moon up above. Ha, ha, ha! Let me tell you about love!"**

"Fingers has a sweetheart," said Gus. "And her name is Ramona."

"He does! Oh, good grief," said Fanny.

Chapter Seventeen

Do Do Da Da

"Let's go patrol the woods," said Fanny.

"Great idea!" said Gus.

They had to weave their way through the mass of tall sword ferns and bramble that had sprung up everywhere. And, even though it hadn't rained in days, they had to dodge the water that still dripped from the thick green moss that clung to the tree branches.

Fanny thought she heard a chipmunk. She stopped Gus and motioned for him to listen. They both raised their heads and sniffed the air.

"That's not a chipmunk," Gus said.

"Maybe it's a squirrel."

"Too big," said Gus. "Maybe it's a deer."

"Maybe its Darla," said Fanny.

The cats hurried through the brush toward Darla, but stopped mid-step when they saw Paul dancing around in a small clearing with another 'possum.

"Oh, my gosh," Fanny whispered.

"Looks like Paul has a girlfriend," said Gus.

"I don't want to sound unkind, but I always thought a lady 'possum would be prettier," said Fanny.

Gus watched Paul and the lady 'possum dancing around the clearing, making smacking and clicking sounds, all the while grinning giddily at each other. "You may not think she's pretty, but Paul seems to think she's beautiful," said Gus.

"Uh-oh," said Fanny. "Paul and his lady have company." The cats stayed stone-still and watched as a 'possum twice the size of Paul stormed into the clearing. It didn't hesitate but put its head down and charged Paul like a bull at a rodeo. The lady 'possum ran away and hid in the bushes. Paul stood his ground but when the big 'possum's head crashed into his side, it send him flying. Poor Paul landed with a thud that knocked the air out of him. He shook his head, drew his lips back, hissed, jumped up, and charged back. The big 'possum had his face in the bushes looking for the lady 'possum, paying no attention to Paul. Paul smacked him head-first in the side. The big guy stumbled, but didn't fall. He swung around, but he was big and slow. Paul jabbed him with his head again then whirled around and got him with a tail slap. They squared off and made hissing sounds. The big 'possum crouched down and charged at Paul, but Paul moved like a well-trained matador and stepped out of the way. The big 'possum charged him again and this time Paul jabbed at him as he stepped out of the way and let the big guy pass.

"I've never seen Paul stand up and fight for something before," Fanny whispered.

"He must really like this girl."

"That other 'possum must really like her too!"

The big 'possum charged back into the clearing. Paul shook his head as if to say, here we go again! Paul was quick, the big 'possum was slow. Paul got his licks in and, after a few more go-arounds, the big

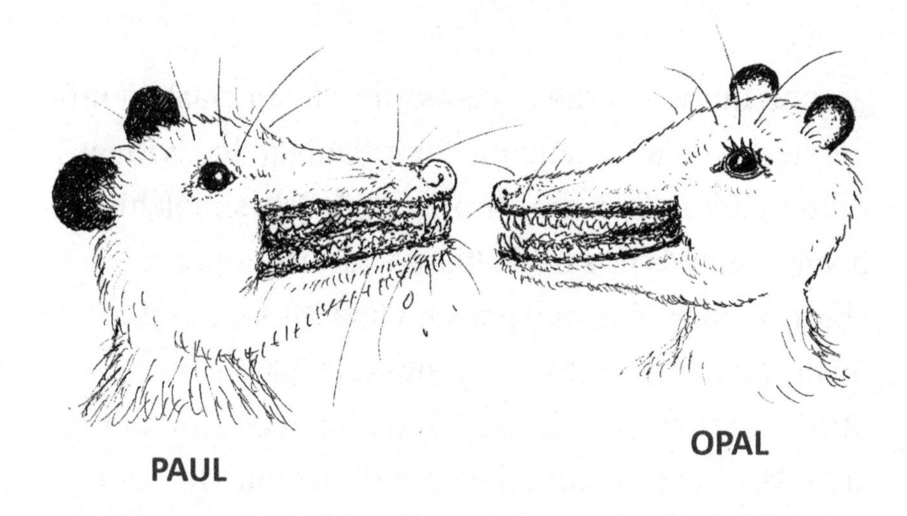

'possum hobbled away. Paul limped on one leg, but when the lady 'possum came out of the bushes and joined him, he stopped limping and held his head high.

Gus and Fanny joined them.

The lady 'possum began side-stepping toward the bushes, but Paul circled around to stop her. He touched her nose to nose and grinned (like only a 'possum can) and said, "It's okay, Opal. This is Gus and Fanny, the cats I was telling you about. Believe it or not, they are my friends."

"Hey Opal," said Gus.

Opal stared at the cats for a moment before replying, "Hey."

"I'm Gus and," he nodded toward Fanny, "this is

Fanny."

"Pleased to meet you," said Fanny.

Suddenly, a squirrel ran up a nearby tree. Fanny shot after it leaving the 'possums staring after her. Gus shrugged. "Catch you later!" he called and followed after her.

The cats spent a lovely afternoon chasing rodents, sunbathing, and simply enjoying the warm spring day. Later that evening, after they had finished eating the kibble in their bowl, Fanny asked Gus, "Weren't you surprised to see Paul in action today, chasing off that 'possum?"

"Not really," said Gus. He touched Fanny nose to nose. "It's spring."

Fanny sat down and groomed the fur on her shoulder. She lifted her head and looked into Gus's eyes and purred.

From inside Hilma's trunk they heard Hilma singing, "Love is in the air, do, do, da, da."

"Oh, good grief," Fanny growled.

Chapter Eighteen

Rappity Rap Rappity Rap

Songbirds twittered. Bees buzzed. Frogs croaked. Crickets chirped. Geese honked. The sounds of spring filled the air!

An explosion of wildflowers in a rainbow of colors covered the farm. Delicate blooms in soft pastels blanketed the apple, pear, peach, and cherry trees. Even the grass was a bright, emerald green. Gus and Fanny were tickled pink that winter was over.

But one bright morning puffy white clouds drifted across the sky making the sun play peek-a-boo. A gentle breeze changed to strong gusts that scattered blossoms off the fruit trees and made the heavy limbs on the tall firs sway back and forth. The clouds started to bunch up and turned a dark gray.

Fanny was squatted down in some tall grass ready to pounce on a grasshopper.

Gus shivered. "I think it's going to rain."

Fanny sprung at the grasshopper, trapping it on the ground. She raised her paw ever so slightly. The grasshopper hopped away. "Hmmm," she said, then crept after it.

The clouds settled all the way to the ground and the wind stopped. A few tiny snowflakes began floating down. "This just can't be happening!" said Gus. More and more snowflakes came down. "It's spring. We can't be having a snowstorm now!"

Fanny gave up hunting and joined Gus. "Brrr," she said. "Come on, let's go back to the barn until this passes. I hate getting wet!"

Gus and Fanny slipped under the barn door, shook the snow from their coats and went to the window and watched the delicate flakes fall. Gus hung his head and moaned, "But it's supposed to be spring."

Fingers and Ramona squeezed in under the barn door and shook the snow flakes from their fur onto each other. Fingers swiped them from his face then gave Ramona a big hug. "Hey, cats! Where's my cut? I told Ramona I'd take her out for a bite ta eat." He gave her another hug. "We're on a date."

Gus was laying on the windowsill, his head down on his paws. "We left your cut in our dish. Help yourselves."

"Why so down in the mouth, my friend?"

"Snow, Fingers." Gus raised his head and looked outside. "It's snowing. I'm done with winter. I want sunshine and flowers."

Fingers and Ramona joined the cats at the window. Fingers stared at the falling snow and yawned. "It's just a little shower. Cheer up. It'll stop soon."

Paul and Opal squeezed under the barn door and stomped their feet. "It's snowing!" said Paul.

"We know," the cats and raccoons said in unison.

"We ducked in here to warm up our feet," said Paul. "We'll be leaving as soon as this shower passes. Mind if we join you?" The cats and raccoons made room for Paul and Opal at the window.

Bud and Petal popped up in the barn from under the door and shook the snow from their fur.

Fanny raised her head and growled, "Monsieur, what did I tell you about bringing Petal to the barn?"

Bud and Petal jumped and held paws. “Oh geez, Fanny,” said Bud. “I didn’t see you there. Petal and me, no, Petal and I, well, we just thought it would be nice to wait out the snow shower in here where it’s dry. It’s snowing. Did you know it’s snowing? Of course you know, you’re all looking out the window at it. Can we stay, just this once, until the snow stops? Is it sticking? It’s not sticking, is it?”

Ramona stuck her nose out the window. Snowflakes piled up on her snout. She pulled her head back in and nuzzled Fingers.

“It ain’t stoppin!” said Fingers.

Gus looked from Fanny to the skunks and said, “Come on in you two, but remember the absolute rule!”

“Absolutely no puffing!” Bud said.

Fanny growled, “Absolutely!”

Bud and Petal joined the others at the window. Cats, raccoons, and ‘possums scrunched a little closer together, moving ever so slightly away from the skunks. They all hung their heads and watched the flakes falling, piling up deeper and deeper.

Gus saw Marvin and Marcia’s little heads pop out from underneath hay bales stacked in the barn’s loft. They twitched their noses and sniffed the air.

"Snow?" Marcia asked.

"Snow!" Marvin answered.

"Snow!" Gus said.

The mice ducked back under the hay.

After a few minutes watching the farm turn a bright white and listening to the soft silence of the spring snow storm, Bud turned to Petal and said, "All this snow is making me sleepy. I guess winter isn't over. We should still be hibernating." Petal hung her head even lower and turned to go.

Fingers shook his head and shouted, "How many times I gotta tell youz, Buddly? Skunks don't hibernate! Geez!"

Petal jumped. Bud stomped his foot. "Whatever, Fingers!" Bud shouted back.

Paul growled and said, "Gus! I thought you said spring was here. This sure looks like winter to me!" He nudged Opal. "Come on, we may as well hibernate, too."

"'possums don't hibernate, either!" Fingers shouted.

Paul poked Fingers. "I say we hibernate!"

"Pauly, youz don't truly hibernate. And don't youz be pokin' me," said Fingers.

Fingers poked Paul pushing him up against Opal, which pushed her up against Bud. Bud reached around Opal and poked Paul, pushing Paul back against Fingers, who pushed up against Gus. Fingers glared at Paul. Paul glared at Bud.

"Hey, everybody!" said Gus. "Stop it! Can't we all just get along? I'm just as disappointed as you. I thought the time for snowstorms was past."

"Humph!" said Fingers.

Bud hung his head and stared at his feet. "Just wake me up when winter is really over."

Paul sighed.

Hilma jetted out of her steamer trunk tugging her red silk scarf behind her. She hovered over her furry friends and screeched, "IS EVERYONE HAVING A BAD

DAY? I don't know when I've seen you all so grumpy, gloomy, and glum. Its just a little spring snowstorm. She threw her head back, cackled, flew to the hayloft, and called, "KIT KAT, COME!"

The ghost cat seeped out of the steamer trunk, swirled around the barn, and settled herself on Hilma's lap.

Hilma screeched, "Doctor Reginald Xavier Gitwell had a cure for gloomy days like this!" She took Kit Kat by her front paws and flew up in the air twirling the ghost cat around and around. "We would have a party and dance and dance and dance! I say we have a good old-fashioned square dance! Who can be sad when you're dancing? Swing your partner, Do-si-do!"

RAP, RAPPITY, RAP, RAP . . . RAP, RAP! came knocks on the barn door. Everyone in the barn turned and watched Finger's brother Handzie, his boss Tony, and cousin Knuckles swagger into the barn.

Fingers gave Tony a salute. "Hey, Boss, whatcha doin' out in this weatha?"

"The boys here," Tony nodded to Handzie and Knuckles, "told me this was where youz been hidin' out." He pointed to Ramona. "Who's your friend there?"

Ramona smiled and waved. Fingers silently scooted a little closer to Ramona.

Tony stomped his feet and brushed the snow off his shoulders. "She's a looker." He scanned the barn. "I see why youz been a-hidin' her."

Ramona giggled.

Suddenly, Hilma swooped down and circled round and round the trio of gangster raccoons. "PERFECT! I need a band!"

"Hey there, Hildy," said Tony. "We're a band alright."

"Yeah," said Knuckles. "A band of gangsters!"

Tony, Knuckles, and Handzie laughed and punched at

each other's shoulders.

"Tonight you gangsters are going to be a band of musicians." She reached for Tony and Knuckles by the scruff of their necks. "I think I'm strong enough to do this now!" She picked them both up and shook them like marionettes.

"This is not cool," said Knuckles.

"Put me down," Tony growled.

Hilma dropped them grumbling and groaning in the hayloft. They both started to scramble out of the loft but Hilma swirled around and through them and, in a creepy, quiet, ghostly voice said, "Stay." Tony and Knuckles stayed.

There was a collective gasp from the cats, raccoons, 'possums, skunks, and even the mice.

"Hallelujah!" She flexed the muscles in her arms and said, "I'm getting stronger every day! One day soon I might be able to leave this barn!"

Hilma went back to the barn floor and grabbed a brown glass jug with one hand and Handzie with the other. Handzie kicked and flailed about as Hilma flew up into the loft with him. "Marvelous!" she said as she dropped Handzie alongside Tony and Knuckles.

She handed Hanzie the jug. "You'll be playing this." Handzie gave Hilma a puzzled look. Tony and Knuckles shrugged their shoulders.

She flew to the work bench and ran her hands over the tools hanging from the wall behind it. Gus watched the tools sway at her touch. He was as mesmerized as everyone else by Hilma's graceful, effortless new strength. Hilma stopped at a carpenter saw and tapped its wooden handle with her long fingernail. She pulled the saw from the wall. "Ah, this will do!"

"Sheesh!" Gus said.

"I know, right!" said Fanny. "She's getting stronger and stronger."

Hilma plucked a small hammer from the wall and took it along with the saw to Tony. "Here, you'll be playing these." Tony held them out in front of himself as though they were deadly snakes.

Hilma grabbed an empty bucket by its bail and dropped it at Knuckle's feet. "And, my furry friend, you'll be playing this." She tipped the bucket over and Knuckles banged it with his knuckles. THUNK. THUNK.

"That's right, Knuckles, but I think we can do much

better than that." She brought him two screw drivers.

"I get it," he said and twirled the screw drivers in the air, caught them, and tapped the bucket. RAT-A-TAT!

"Tony, you look confused," said Hilma. She guided his hand with the hammer to tap the saw he held in his other. It made an eerie sound. OOWWEEEEOO!

Handzie grinned and winked at Hilma. "Me! Me! What do I do with this?" He held out the jug.

"That's the spirit, Handzie! Put your lips together and blow into the jug," said Hilma.

Handzie blew into the jug. WHOMP, WHOMP, WHOMP! "Cool," he said.

Hilma stood at the edge of the hayloft, cackled, clapped her ghostly hands, and sang out, "Follow my lead, boys! We're going to make some music! You all are a barnyard jug band now! Yahoo!" And, to the rest of the animals in the barn, she shouted, "Now, all you grumpy couples form a circle. You're about to have some fun!"

No one moved a muscle; they simply stared at Hilma. "Come on, now!" she sang out. She turned to Tony and started humming a tune. Tony tapped the saw to the beat, then Handzie and Knuckles joined in. She flew to the cats, 'possums, raccoons, and skunks and arranged them in pairs in a circle on the barn floor.

Opal fainted.

"Tich, tich," Hilma said to Paul. "The rest of you, bow to your partner! Circle left!" Hilma sang out. She nudged Fanny and winked at Gus. "Circle left! Curtsy and turn."

At first the couples were clumsy. They didn't know their right from their left or what a curtsy even was but as the music played and Hilma called and sang they were soon prancing around the floor, kicking up their heels, singing and laughing.

Hilma flew back to the hayloft to get a bird's-eye view and called "Do-si-do! Forward and back!" Tony and the gang wailed on their musical instruments and stomped their feet. All the couples except the opossums were laughing, clapping, and swaying around on the barn floor. Hilma joined them swinging Kit Kat by her paws. "Four ladies chain! Now, promenade!"

Marvin and Marcia took each other's paws and danced around and around the loft.

Paul picked up Opal's paw and shook it. "Ah, Opal,

honey, I need a dance partner," he pleaded. "Opal!"

"Come down the middle!" Hilma called.

Bud and Petal were dancing and smiling into each other's eyes when Bud tripped over Opal and fell down taking Petal with him. The skunks got up laughing. "Do-si-do!" they sang.

Hilma twirled with Kit Kat over to Paul and sang, "Swing your partner UP OFF the floor! No really, Paul. We can't have an 'possum playing 'possum in the middle of our dance floor!"

Everyone laughed. Bud, Fingers, Gus and Marvin swung their partners. Paul drug Opal to the side of the barn.

A pair of squirrels peeked in the window. They listened and watched the hullabaloo of the raccoon band and dancers for several seconds. Finally, one squirrel looked at the other and said, "These guys are nuts!"

Hilma called, "Now, promenade!"

Opal woke up. Paul took her paws and they joined the others. "Whoo-hoo!" he sang. "Now we can promenade!"

All the animals were enjoying themselves, forgetting

the cold snow outside, when suddenly there came a long, high-pitched, rising howl followed by yips and yelps from just outside the barn door.

"COYOTES!" Gus yelled.

Chapter Nineteen

Howl Howl

Hilma became a ghostly blur as she streaked across the barn. She craned her neck out of the window and screeched, "Coyotes!"

The jug band stopped playing, the couples quit dancing, and the singing and laughter died away.

A pack of shaggy coyotes were outside circling the barn. It wasn't long before a pair of the monsters made their way into the lean-to shed. Bud whispered, "This is bad!"

The wing-like, lean-to shed, built up against the barn, was open on three sides like a carport. There was a door and two windows between the main barn and the lean-to. The windows had no glass or screen but that wasn't the problem. The problem was the door. It was closed but there was no latch, only two big metal barrels standing up against it kept it shut. If the coyotes jumped at it, over and over, the door just might open.

Fingers grabbed Ramona by her shoulders and said, "RRRRRRRRamona, rrrrrrrun!"

Ramona gazed into Fingers' eyes and said, "Ah, Fingers, Honey . . . you gotta be kidding." She waddled to the lean-to window. Fingers hurried over to join her and bumped into a dusty golf bag knocking it over. The clubs slid out and clanked to the floor. The golf balls were set free and rolled every which way.

"That's the ticket," said Ramona, as she scrambled after a ball wheeling past Finger's foot. They reached for the ball at the same time and clunked heads.

Fingers stood up rubbing his noggin. Ramona snatched the ball and threw it out the window. "Take that!" she roared. One of the coyotes yipped and ran away.

Fingers gave her a crooked smile and raised his paw to high-five. Ramona slapped his paw and batted her eyes at him.

Coyotes gathered at window on the other side of the barn.

Tony was standing in the loft watching the action. Hilma flew past him and whispered in his ear, "Do-si-do."

He shook his head and said, "Do-si-do, all right." He jumped to the barn floor, clapped his paws together, and yelled, "Yo, Fingers, pick up one of those sticks and whack a ball over here to me."

"Right, Boss," said Fingers. He picked up a golf club

and examined it for a second. "I've never used one of these before."

"Come on, come on," Tony said impatiently.

"Okay, Boss." Fingers gripped the handle, extended the long metal club out in front of himself, and set it down alongside a bright yellow golf ball. He shifted his weight from foot to foot, looked from the ball to Tony and then lifted the club back and swung. "Crack," the club smacked the ball and it rocketed across the room to Tony.

"Fanny, duck!" Gus yelled as the ball whizzed past her head. Tony snatched the ball out of the air and hurled it out the window hitting one of the coyotes in the paw. It yiked and ran away yipping.

"That's the ticket," Ramona said again.

"Easy peasy," said Tony.

Fanny hurried to Gus's side. They heard coyote feet pounding on the big barn door. Faster than a speeding bullet, Bud was at the door and lifting his tail.

Gus gasped and yelled, "No! Bud!" The cats hurried to the little skunk before he sprayed and Gus jerked his tail down. "Not in the barn! Never in the barn!"

Bud hung his head and stepped away. Gus wanted to comfort Bud, but there was no time. He swiped at the coyote paw reaching under the door. The coyote growled, but kept digging. Fanny sprung at its paw and this time it left howling. Fanny lifted her paw and grinned at the blood that dripped from her claw.

Gus and Fanny dashed from door to door batting and clawing at coyotes trying to get in. Bud and Petal started running in a tight circle, stomping, hissing and squealing at the top of their lungs. Paul and Opal made their own loud clicking, squawking and hissing sounds. Paul even hopped up on the window sill, drew his lips back in a fierce grin showing all 52 of his needle-sharp teeth and drooled.

"Get outta my way, Paulie," said Fingers. "Youz in the strike zone." He nudged Paul. Paul lost his balance and would have fallen out the window but Fingers grabbed him and yanked him back inside. "Whoops!"

Opal hurried to Paul and asked, "Pauly Wog, are you okay?" She motioned for him to follow her as she crawled under the tractor. "Come here. Let me check you over."

Fingers climbed up into the hayloft and then out onto the lean-to roof. He came back inside and yelled down to Tony, "Hey, toss some a those golf balls up here. The coyotes are easy pickins from up here!"

"Gotcha, Fingers," Tony said.

Knuckles and Handzie were just sitting together in the hayloft watching all the action. Tony yelled, "It's fire brigade time, boys," and lobbed a golf ball up to them. Knuckles reached out and snagged it out of the air.

Fingers waved to Knuckles and then climbed out to the lean-to roof. "Right, fire brigade time, I get it," said Knuckles. He poked Handzie in the shoulder and said, "Get over to the wall there. I'll pass the balls to you after Tony sends them up. You pass them on to Fingers out there. Handzie waddled over and turned to Knuckles. Knuckles wound up and threw a fast ball. The ball smacked in Handzie's paw with a loud crack. Handzie glared at Knuckles, blew on his paws, and then passed the ball to Fingers.

Fingers hummed as he waddled back and forth on the roof. Handzie passed him ball after ball and Fingers hurled them at the coyotes. "Easy peasy!" he yelled.

Gus saw Fanny's tail sticking out between some boxes stacked in the back stanchion and went to her. "There's a coyote digging right outside this wall," she said.

Gus peered out between the boards of the wall. What he saw was a lone coyote, darker in color than the rest of the coyotes in the pack, nearly all black. It was digging at the base of the wall, a flood of dirt flying out behind it with each scrape of its big paws. It looked up and their eyes locked. "You think you're safe in there?" it said.

Gus shook with anger. He was thinking about what he could do when, WHAM, a potato slammed down on the coyote's back.

"Yee haw!" Ramona yelled. "I hit him square." The coyote yipped and ran. Ramona scurried back to a box of potatoes she'd found at the back of the barn and plucked another spud from it. She hurried back to the window and waited for the next coyote unlucky enough to be within her range.

Gus and Fanny let out a nervous laugh. They started to leave the stanchion when Gus turned to Fanny and said, "If those coyotes get in here; if they make it past the raccoons . . . .."

"That's not going to happen, Gus."

"If they make it into the barn," Gus continued. "Get up into the loft. Don't stay down here."

"You don't have to worry about me."

Gus touched Fanny's nose with his. "But I do."

There was a loud thud on the big barn doors and Gus streaked over to it.

If the coyotes get in here, if they make it past the raccoons, please don't be the brave Master Guard Cat, Gus, Fanny thought watching him.

Gus put his face up to the crack and bristled when he found himself looking into the eyes of the most monstrous coyote of the bunch. The big fellow was just sitting there on his haunches with his chest all puffed out. He blinked his golden eyes at Gus and then raised his snout straight up in the air and let out a loud howl.

Gus jerked back away from the door and croaked,

"Whoa!" But he quickly put his face back to the crack to watch, spellbound by the majesty of the big animal.

The coyote stood up and shook, sending snow flying off his furry coat. He turned his gaze back on Gus and said, "I'll be back."

"Whoa!" Gus said again. "Not if we can help it."

The big guy reared up then galloped away. Moments later the rest of the pack of coyotes loped past the door following their leader.

All activity inside the barn stopped. They all looked at one another, listening. It wasn't more than a minute or two later that, off in the distance, the air was filled with the long rising and falling note of a single coyote's howl followed by the shrill yi-yis and yip-yips of the rest of the pack. It happened again and again, but each time the sounds were coming from farther and farther away.

It was Handzie who finally broke the silence in the barn. "Whoop! Whoop! Whoop!" he yelled. Knuckles and Fingers let out a whoop, too, and the three of them climbed down from the loft. Tony, Gus, and Bud cheered and patted each other on the back.

Hilma cackled. "See what I told you, there's nothing like a good old-fashion square dance to shake off the doldrums of a gray day! Come, Kit Kat." They seeped back into her trunk.

"Oh yeah, we took care of those guys!" said Knuckles. There was more cheering and chest bumping as the raccoons congratulated each other.

Gus was relieved that they'd gone, but he couldn't relax. "Phew, I've never seen coyotes act like that before," he said. "How long before they return? The big guy, he said he'd be back."

"Don't youz worry 'bout them!" said Tony.

"Why do you suppose they were acting like that?" Gus asked.

"They're after easy prey. They're after the babies," said Tony. "This happens every spring." He thumped Gus on the shoulder.

Fingers twirled the gold ring around on his finger and began restlessly searching about the barn.

"You lookin' for that beauty, Ramona?" Tony asked.

"Yes Sir, I am," said Fingers.

"I saw her sneakin' out right after the coyotes left."

"Rrrrrrrona!" Fingers cried and climbed out the lean -to window.

Bud looked nervously around for Petal and saw her standing among some boxes. "We should go now," he called to her.

"Okay Budkins," said Petal. The skunks followed Fingers.

Paul and Opal climbed out from under the tractor. Paul saluted Gus and they quietly left the barn.

"We'll be seein' youz, Gus," said Tony. And, without further ado, Tony, Knuckles and Handzie waddled out the barn.

Gus sat down in the middle of the barn. "Babies," he said and shook his head. "I should have known that."

He wandered back among the boxes looking for Fanny. She wasn't there. He yowled. Fanny yowled back from the loft. He found her tucked down between two bales of hay and wiggled his way in beside her. She moaned.

"What's wrong?" Gus asked. "Are you hurt?"

Fanny squirmed out and sprawled on top of the hay. "No, I'm not hurt. I just feel kind of queasy."

"Is there anything I can do?"

"No, I'll be fine. I just want to go to sleep until this passes."

Gus lay down alongside her and soon Fanny fell asleep. But Gus couldn't sleep. He kept thinking about the coyotes. He could still hear their yips, yelps, and yi-yis fading as they moved farther and farther away from the farm. He kept an eagle eye out scanning the barn until finally his head drooped and he fell asleep. Some time later it was the sound of rain pounding on the roof that woke him. He raised his head. Fanny was gone. Then he heard a mewing sound. He tiptoed to the edge of the loft and strained his ears to listen. He whispered, "Fanny?"

Chapter Twenty

Mew Mew

"YOW!" It was Fanny's unmistakable scream and it was coming from the barn floor.

Gus scrambled down from the loft to search for her. He heard the yip of a coyote. *Not again,* he thought. The fur along his back stood straight up. He whispered, "Fanny! Where are you?"

"GUS!" Fanny yowled.

Gus finally spotted her in a cardboard box in a corner of the barn. She was curled protectively around six tiny kittens with a look of terror on her face. "Gus,"

Fanny pleaded, "Help us!"

The coyote was right on the other side of the wall. He was digging at the boards with his massive paws making the crack between the boards larger.

Gus had little time to think. Instinctively, he sprung out the side window and ran around the barn to face the coyote head on. It was the same black coyote that had been digging at the side of the barn earlier. It lunged at Gus, but Gus veered away. Assuming victory, the coyote went back to digging, but Gus wasn't about to give up. He swiped the coyote's tail with his sharp claws. The coyote yipped and turned to face Gus once again. "You think you can stop me, cat?" he snarled.

Gus had to do something different in order to get rid of this beast. He reared up, hissed and gave him a one-two swipe with both paws then turned and ran and hoped the coyote would chase after him.

The coyote didn't hesitate. He rocketed after Gus like a tightly stretched rubber band being let loose. "You've asked for it now. You're toast, pussy cat!" he yelled.

Gus sprinted across the old garden and then the road. He jetted through the grass of a wide, open meadow. *Come on, you mangy coyote, follow me!* The coyote ran fast and strong, but Gus was nimble and could zigzag away from him. The raindrops hitting Gus's face made it hard for him to see. But he struggled on even though the muscles in his legs were hurting and he could hardly catch his breath. The tireless coyote inched closer and closer. Gus thought, *I can stop here and take my chances with the beast or keep running and climb into that apple tree just ahead.* Gus knew there was no choice; he had to make it up into that tree. He charged ahead. He made it to the tree with the coyote only inches behind him. Gus scrambled up the tree trunk. The coyote reached up and caught the tip of Gus's tail and bit down. Gus buried his claws into the tree's bark and hung on. *You're not getting me!* He thought. He jerked away with all his might and shot up the tree leaving the coyote with a mouth full of fur. Gus's heart was pounding and he was breathing too hard to even growl or hiss at the coyote.

Gus was just out of the coyote's reach. "You think climbing this wimpy tree is going to save you?" The brute jumped, growled, yipped and even bit chunks of bark from the tree. "I'll get you!" he yelled. But

finally he collapsed in a heap at the base of the tree. His tongue lolled out of the side of his mouth. He was panting rapidly. Gus knew he was safe up there, but how long would he have to wait for the coyote to leave? Or would it leave at all? As it turned out, he didn't have to wait long. The coyote fell asleep. Gus thought, *this is my chance,* and started inching his way down the tree when off in the distance came the clear, loud, distinctive coyote howl of that massive, yellow-eyed coyote that Gus had heard before. The coyote under the tree stirred and shot to attention. “Yes sir!” he called, then threw his head back and howled. “I’m on my way, sir!” Gus froze. The coyote ran away without so much as a look back, and, much to Gus’s relief, he was not running in the direction of the barn.

Gus waited in the tree for another moment or two just to be sure the coyote was not coming back. And then it hit him. *Kittens!* He thought. *Kittens! I’m a daddy!*

The End

Made in the USA
Columbia, SC
25 January 2024

30115860R00085